KISS THE RAIN

By the Author

Visit us at www.boldstrokesbooks.com

KISS THE RAIN

by

Larkin Rose

2011

KISS THE RAIN

© 2011 By Larkin Rose. All Rights Reserved.

ISBN 10: 1-60282-211-5
ISBN 13: 978-1-60282-211-5

This Trade Paperback Original Is Published By
Bold Strokes Books, Inc.
P.O. Box 249
Valley Falls, NY 12185

First Edition: March 2011

CREDITS

EDITOR: CINDY CRESAP
PRODUCTION DESIGN: STACIA SEAMAN
COVER DESIGN BY SHERI (GRAPHICARTIST2020@HOTMAIL.COM)

Dedication

Jove. Thank you a thousand times, and I freaking miss you!

Toni. You're an amazing friend and grandma. I don't know what I'd do without you.

Barbara Karmazin. You will never, ever, be forgotten. Thank you for my wings.

Rose. Fifteen years and counting. You're still the one.

Finally, to my mother, Linda, who went to sleep with the angels. I love you. To the moon and back.

CHAPTER ONE

"What are you wearing, my sexy Eve?"

Eve Harris welcomed the familiar tightening of her insides in response to Lexi's question. She wasn't normally a sucker for sexy accents, but the way the mellifluous British rolled smoothly off Lexi's tongue was a different matter. Her voice alone was orgasmic. The accent, laced with erotic commands, jerked Eve to screaming spasms with every phone call to her personal sex operator. She tucked the phone closer to her ear. "Jeans and an old ratty Ozzy Osbourne T-shirt."

"Mmm. I would have never guessed. You don't strike me as a heavy-metal headbanger," Lexi said.

Eve chuckled and snuggled deeper into the pillows on her bed while eyeing the bright blue vibrator lying in wait beside her. She fingered its silicone length. "There's a lot you don't know about me."

"True, but I know the most important thing."

"Oh yeah, what's that?"

"I know what you sound like when you come, screaming my name." Lexi's voice dropped into that husky tone she used just before she started commanding Eve to touch and finger herself, to fuck herself with the very toy she'd insisted Eve purchase.

Eve swallowed a moan while her pussy clamped into a painful vise. Those commands were what kept her dialing Lexi's private sex line every spare minute her busy life allowed. Her time was at a premium with almost every priceless hour of daylight spent poring over new clothing designs. From choosing the right material to create the perfect drape, crinkle, or crease, to matching colors, coordinated accessories, and jewelry for that flawless finishing touch. Eve inhaled her career. Craved it, in fact. There was nothing more satisfying than watching a new design evolving into reality, every stitch breathing life into the gorgeous fabrics she sourced from around the globe.

Well, she thought things were satisfying until she'd stumbled into a stranger while in London for fashion week two years ago. The woman had been ridiculously femme—whore-red lipstick with her matching dangerous nails caressing long, perfect curls as one would a loving pet, and a pearl necklace leading a path to an almost nonexistent cleavage. Eve had recoiled with a shudder, not her type at all. She just couldn't do femme, and this woman screamed lipstick lesbian. She was tall with high cheekbones and plump, naturally pouty lips.

They both sat alone in a smoke-filled nightclub and eventually struck up a conversation. To save from yelling over the music, they made their way down the length of bar stools as the subjects ranged from life, careers, and the most dreaded of all, love. Eve wasn't into love. She'd been there, drowned in it, and never wanted to revisit its lack of life preservers again. Her scarce time didn't allow for coddling or wooing some hug-hungry "spend all of your waking moments with me" woman. There just wasn't time to devote to sulky, whimpering partners who pouted because Eve's career always came before them.

Eve had been fascinated to learn the woman shared her peeves about dating, how people were always looking for love instead of running from it, putting themselves second to bow to a partner's needs. That kind of life was for her mother, not Eve. Her mother had subscribed to being the best little housewife and mother she could be while her father climbed the rungs of a successful career ladder. As her father had, Eve moved hell and earth to be at the top, to rise above all else. Except she hadn't left a little missus behind to raise a family along the journey.

The woman giggled while Eve related horrendous stories of old flames, how every relationship seemed to die a slow, agonizing death long before the sex had burned out. Sex. It was all about the sex for Eve. Why did stable sex have to come with a price tag? Her undivided attention? Her companion had laughed, agreeing with every word.

"I must go. It's been refreshing meeting someone with the same values about life and love." She scribbled something on a napkin and handed it to Eve. "You'll find all you need with a single phone call. Her name is Lexi. She's the complete package. All you have to do is dial the number. She'll take care of the rest. Utter discretion and no strings attached."

Eve had taken the napkin to study the numbers, curious as to who this beauty was pimping out, or exactly what she was pimping out. She found two sets of digits.

"The bottom number is my cell. I'm Zara Manis, by the way. My daddy is Phillip Manis." Zara delicately held out her hand as if Eve should recognize the name and kiss the ivory flesh.

Instead, Eve shook her hand like a business acquaintance. First, she didn't bother with such unimportant things as well-known names on foreign soil, no matter how much they spent on her designs. Second, she'd be damned if she fawned over someone who already had herself on a pedestal. "It was great to meet you. I'm Eve."

"I know who you are, Eve Harris. I'm a huge fan and rarely miss the fashion events. I happen to be in town this week to visit my daddy. He spoils me so. Especially during fashion week. Lucky you." She leaned toward Eve and whispered, "I'll be sitting in the front row, and I won't be wearing underwear."

Stupefied, Eve begged her mind to find a respectful rejection. Zara was all femme. So was Eve. That combination didn't fly. And neither did sleeping with the daughter of a man whose wallet seemed as deep as space.

"We have too much in common not to fuck and walk our separate ways, Eve." Zara gave a sinfully sweet smile. "Give me a try. I can be as hard as any butch you desire." She squeezed Eve's hand. "Friday night, right after the finale dinner at La Pierre Hotel, Royal Suite. I promise to make it worth your while."

She sashayed out of the club on spiked stilettos, leaving Eve stunned and uncharacteristically curious.

Like the idiot she'd fought hard to never be, curiosity had led Eve to Zara's hotel suite, and against her better judgment, to her bed. Their one-week relationship was nothing more than passing lust between two people who shared the same beliefs—that women could fuck and be fucked and walk away with their heads held high after lust ran cold. However, Eve couldn't even say she'd been in lust. Quite the opposite. They'd both somehow gotten caught up in the whirlwind abnormal sex. Or so it was for Eve.

Those quick fucks had been more than enough. She had fucked her clone, minus the high-maintenance. Sharing fashion tips and designer dresses with a femme proved utterly disturbing.

It had also proved a salutary lesson. Proved she was a genuine butch lover who didn't play well with other femmes. Eve vowed she would never fuck another female with fingernails the length of deadly weapons for as long as she lived.

Now here she lay in her Manhattan apartment, long after grabbing hold of her scarred sanity and promising to maintain a friendship with Zara, which she'd done, her pussy hot and needy, yet more satisfied than she believed could be possible, with Lexi giving her everything her body craved from across the map.

Zara had been right about one thing: Lexi was the complete package. They barely shared personal or business matters, didn't exchange sweet nothings, though on occasion they'd swap some private tidbit about themselves. She knew Lexi lived in London, that there was no food she wouldn't try, and she loved walking in the rain. Lexi knew that Eve lived in Manhattan and worked nonstop, that she ate nutrition bars for breakfast and lunch and sometimes dinner too if time didn't allow her a hot meal, and that she hated the rain. There were no arguments, no sharing bed space, no fighting over something as ridiculous as a toothpaste lid or which way the toilet paper should unwind, and best of all, no simpering females fighting for her attention. Lexi was perfect, and she made Eve's life complete. Eve reveled in the hot, heavenly, and erotically challenging sex, and succumbed willingly to reversing her powerhouse role with every call, with every command easily given in that risqué accent.

Lexi made her feel connected to her otherwise disconnected sex life, as if she were lying right beside her, inside her, teasing, stroking, and drawing out a satisfying orgasm with skilled hands.

"I need to hear you come, Eve."

Eve closed her eyes and let Lexi's description of herself float inside her mind. Tall, with broad shoulders, six-pack abs glistening after a heavy workout, short brown hair that she towel-dried and left disheveled. The image ended with ivy green eyes staring down over her. Eve's temperature spiked as the illusion blossomed. Lexi had described her fantasy woman, and now, Eve wanted to fuck that 3-D image while the voice of reality stroked her to convulsions.

"Then make me." Eve fanned her legs open and closed, anxious, desperate for those commands.

"Unsnap your jeans."

Eve did as she was told, ripping at the button and tearing down the zipper with desperate tugs. She didn't dare take her jeans off. She'd learned the hard way that disobeying Lexi's commands could be brutal. Lexi could withhold an orgasm as easy as pressing a button to cut the phone connection.

"Done."

"Slip your hand inside."

Eve worked her hand down until she found her swollen clit. She gently massaged herself, afraid Lexi would hear the catch in her breath. "Okay."

"Don't you dare flick yourself."

"I didn't—wouldn't. I won't." Eve stilled her fingers, her body a mass of nerves and her insides clenching.

"I don't believe you, my horny little workaholic. I need you to push that hand farther down, away from that tight, sensitive clit, and drive those fingers inside. Tell me how wet you are, Eve."

Eve pressed two fingers inside herself, easing the heels of her bare feet against the mattress for leverage and thrusting against the palm of her hand. "I'm soaked…need relief, Lexi. Soon."

Lexi chuckled. "You always need relief. Isn't that why you call me? Isn't that what I give you?"

"Yes. Shit, yes." Eve pumped her hips and thrust deeper, needing to be free from the denim constricting her movements.

"How does it feel, Eve? Tell me."

"Good. It feels so damn good. I need more, Lexi. Please!"

"Not yet. It's not time. With your free hand, raise that middle-school garb over those delicious tits of yours. Free them one at a time, over the top of your bra. I want you looking like a two-bit slut before I let you come."

Eve shoved the T-shirt up to her throat and yanked the edge of her bra down, freeing each breast as told. Her nipples puckered under the cool apartment air, and she couldn't resist pinching one between her fingers. A spark of fire corded in her pussy, and she bucked against her hand.

"I'm so fucking horny."

"Stop!"

Eve growled but stilled her thrusts. She unscrewed her eyes and looked down the length of her body. Indeed, she looked like a two-bit slut, her shirt up, her tits out, and her hand down her pants. Instead of the sight repulsing her, it only made her hornier, and against her better judgment, she pressed her fingers inside herself once again and let out a mew of pleasure.

"I heard that, naughty girl. That'll cost you a few minutes," Lexi scolded her. "Remove your hand."

Eve huffed and jerked her hand from her pants. "I couldn't help it. I'm on fire."

"Silence!"

Eve clamped her jaw tight, her pussy a fire pit. If only her sex life had been like this in reality all these years, she wouldn't be spending a tiny fortune on international calls. Maybe she would have skipped out on work to spend time on a relationship. In bed, of course.

As long as Lexi answered that call, she'd never have to face the cold, hard facts that this kind of sex life didn't exist outside this bedroom, beyond this telephone. Panic nipped at her mind. What if that day came? The day Lexi didn't answer the line. The day Lexi didn't exist.

As quickly as the thought rose, she shoved it back in place. So what if Lexi vanished? Like fish in the sea, there were more Lexis where this one came from. Oh, but could they dare be as deliciously naughty as this one?

"Push your jeans and undies down around your ankles."

Eve shoved and kicked the jeans until the bunched material locked her ankles together. "Okay."

"Show me what you look like. Let me see you through your eyes."

"I look exactly how you wanted me to look—like your two-bit slut." The sight of her body, exposed and open and vulnerable, ankles shackled in place, made Eve miserably horny. "I look like I was fucked in haste."

"You think fucking in haste makes you look like a slut?" Lexi's voice dipped to an animalistic purr. "I'd fuck you in haste. I like fucking."

Eve swallowed hard and her pussy stung. "And I'd let you."

"Where's that silky-smooth dildo, Eve?"

"Right beside me."

"Pick it up. Lick the head."

Eve did as told, her body coming dangerously alive with the anticipation of filling herself. She spread her legs wider and awaited her next command.

"Are you ready, Eve?"

❖

Jodi, otherwise known as Lexi in her role of fantasy artist, trapped the phone between her shoulder and ear as she tugged on a pair of tuxedo pants.

"I want you to spread wide, Eve, but first, I want you to drag the dildo over your crotch and clit. Do not enter until I say so. Do you understand me?"

"Yes. Shit, this feels so good."

Jodi pulled her stiff white shirt on and buttoned the cuffs while Eve panted and whimpered. "That's it, baby, tease yourself. Close your eyes, Eve, feel me driving inside you, thrusting you against the mattress, shoving you toward the edge. You feel so good. Taste so sweet."

Eve hissed. "I'm so close."

Jodi had to admit, of the three remaining clients who had her private sex line, Eve was her favorite. Something about the way Eve cried out grabbed at her and made her close her eyes in dreamy lust. She wasn't attached by any means, always kept the calls as sexual as possible, and just as distant. Well, besides the rare times they'd shared a few personal things, like the fact that she loved the rain. Why the hell had she told Eve that particular fact? Not even her best friend Amelia knew why she lived for its cold dampness. Because it made her feel whole and clean and pure.

"Do you feel me, Eve? My weight pinning you down, my thighs bunched tight as I drive inside you. As I fuck you."

"I feel you…thrusting, pumping. I feel your sweat. Fuck me, Lexi. I'm begging." Eve's breathing was erratic.

Indeed, she was close. Lexi knew the pattern, knew exactly when

Eve would lose control. She'd never forget that first phone call, Eve shy as she stammered, embarrassed, anxious to finish their phone call. Soft persuasion soon had Eve crying out over the line, the sweetest cries she'd ever heard.

"What am I doing to you, Eve?" Jodi sat on the end of the bed and put her shiny black shoes on. She was running behind for her date—a woman who'd paid handsomely for an escort. Jodi wasn't ashamed of who she was. The path she chose in life had kept her off the street corners at fifteen after her mother's death had left her alone in London, a foreign land, far away from her birthplace in Dallas, Texas. Being a military brat, always moving from state to state, country to country, she rarely had time to make deep connections with friends. This life had kept food in her belly, had kept her alive, and for that she'd never hang her head in shame. She'd outlived the hard knocks of life, survived grabbing an hour of shut-eye under bridges with the other homeless when safety allowed, dodging perverts who wouldn't hesitate to rip away a teenager's innocence, and stealing morsels of food from the sidewalk vendors. Thankfully, she'd landed a job as a phone sex operator, immediately adopting the British accent—a subtle mix of south London where she lived first and the more cultured voices of the media. The women ate it up.

It was that first job, in a tiny cubicle of an office with long desks and multiple telephones where she'd met Amelia, her only true friend, then and now. She could well imagine what she looked like—like a lost soul, hungry and desperate. Six months later, she was able to afford a rank little apartment with no heating or cooling. It was a roof over her head, and for that, she was grateful. Amelia had ducked out of that line of work after a couple of years, begging Jodi to take flight with her. Something had told Jodi to stay. She was good at her job, at pleasing the clients. Somehow, she knew exactly what they yearned for. What they wanted, she had. Soon, women requested her by name. The calls rushed in, all wanting her sexy mixed accent and cool manners to rip away their composure for a few minutes.

Now, here she sat, some twenty years later, Amelia still the most important person in her life. Jodi lived in a beautiful city, very similar to the one Eve looked out on every day of her life, and she owned the entire fifteen-story condo building in which she had her apartment plus a fat bank account to ensure she'd never go hungry again.

"You're fucking me...God, fucking me so hard, so deep. Fuck me, Lexi. Please. Please. Let me fill myself."

"I like it when you beg. It's so erotic. Too bad I'm not ready for you to come. And too bad you disobeyed an order."

Jodi checked the clock on the nightstand. Ten more minutes, tops. Her date wouldn't be happy if she arrived late. Tonight, she'd be escorting Carlotta Tate down the red carpet, then fucking her before the stroke of midnight.

"I...uh! You're mean. I'm dying here."

"Can't have that now, can we? Let's see what we can do to remedy your little situation."

"Lexi! Stop teasing me."

"Okay, my sweet, spread those lips for me." Jodi tied her shoe and braced herself. "Slow and easy, enter that delicious pussy. I bet you're so wet. I can almost feel you clenching around my fingers."

Eve gave that helpless cry that wove ribbons of heat through Jodi's crotch. She clenched her jaw against the intensity. The whimpers always awoke something deep inside her, as if Eve held the key to her inner soul.

"Oh, fuck. I'm so close, Lexi."

Jodi lay back on the bed and focused on the spinning ceiling fan. "Flick your clit. Small circles."

Eve whimpered.

"That's it, baby. Faster now. Keep driving that dildo inside. Deep and slow. I bet you look so sexy right now, naked, legs wide, those hardened nipples kissing the air."

"Keep talking. Shit, I can feel you inside me, Lexi."

"Yes, that's me inside you. I'm fucking you. Flick faster, Eve. Let me hear you come."

Eve's breathing hitched and Jodi knew she was close. So fucking close.

"Oh, God, Lexi."

Jodi screwed her eyes shut while prickles of pain seared her pussy. The sound of her name flying off those lips drew her into the intimate moment like a vortex. She caught her hand moving down between her legs. She needed relief. Needed to join Eve so bad it was frightening.

She jerked her hand away just as her fingers curled over her crotch. No attachments! Absolutely no masturbating with a client. It was Rona's first rule before she'd whisked Jodi out of the life of being a sex phone operator and into the exotic realms of being an escort.

Fuck! She wanted to so damn bad, needed to accompany Eve as she cascaded into the erotic abyss.

"I'm coming. Ohmygodohmygodohmygod!"

Jodi fisted her hands against her thighs as Eve whimpered, tortured by those sweet cries.

CHAPTER TWO

Jodi waited for the driver to open her door before she stepped out of the limo. She took in the paparazzi armed with their cameras, clumped in groups outside the golden ropes lining the red carpet. The flashes lit up the night sky as soon as she turned to extend her hand for Carlotta. At the ripe age of fifty-seven, Carlotta, the grande dame of the theater world, had lost none of the grace, sophistication, or style for which she'd become famous. Her air of arrogance kept most people at arm's length. She liked her life private. Her money paid for just that.

Jodi took her red silk-gloved wrist and escorted Carlotta from the stretch limo. Carlotta's personal designer, Navarro, had outdone himself for this occasion, producing the most amazing chiffon gown covered with chips of mirrored glass that glinted like a myriad of diamonds in the flashlights. Carlotta pasted her bright public smile firmly in place while Jodi placed a hand at the small of her back and urged her to the edge of the carpet. The prisms danced as the camera flashes sparkled. Jodi held her head high as she looked over Carlotta's awaiting fans. She never smiled. It kept her expression mysterious, and she liked that.

The actress in front of them moved forward. Slowly, Jodi led her wealthy date onto the red carpet. The crowd shouted, and applause built all around. Shutters hummed ferociously, and then Jodi stepped to the side while the paparazzi beckoned their star to pose for the customary photographs. No doubt the pictures would grace the front covers of every tabloid and newspaper by morning light with their taglines pondering the mysterious date escorting the famous theater director into the limelight. Again. How close they were to the truth. How close they always were. Carlotta had paid handsomely for Jodi's services, not the first time, and surely not the last. But not just any escort—a paid, personal escort who did more than just walk her dates down the velvet aisle, or waltz the rich around a dance floor for her paycheck. She wasn't ashamed. Never had been and never would be.

If anything, Jodi was proud of herself for finding another route out of an otherwise shameful life. She could have ended up in the clutches of a violent pimp, dependent on him for the drugs that made her sordid life bearable, or worse, with her throat slashed and her body dumped in an alley before her eighteenth birthday.

Of course, a personal escort was little removed from a paid whore, but no matter how many ways she examined the formula, Jodi couldn't hang her head in shame. She was alive and living a stylish life. That was far more than she could say about the alternative.

When Carlotta looked her way, the sign that she had given the media enough of her time, Jodi moved back to her side. Carlotta tucked her hand around Jodi's elbow, and together they moved forward. Jodi never held hands with her dates, no matter how big the paycheck. It was too personal. She saved those precious moments for "real" dates. She rarely had those, but she wasn't against finding Ms. Right. Deep down, she was a hopeless romantic just waiting for the breath to be knocked from her lungs when true love whisked into her world. That person would come along eventually. This she knew.

The silver screen might be full of fiction, but romance was real. Her mother was proof of that fact. She'd died with a broken heart, had taken her love to the grave, alongside her husband. She'd never gotten over his death. Even moving herself and her only child back to London, her homeland, couldn't mend the pieces of her shattered life, though she'd tried hard to give Jodi a loving life as a single mother. Jodi could tell things weren't the same, that they probably never would have been had she not been killed in a car accident. Jodi thought of her often, how they talked of her father. Her mother had never let a day pass without speaking of him, how he loved them both dearly, how she would see him one day and hold his hand again. The memories made her smile. Made her yearn for that same unconditional love her mother and father shared.

With no living relatives, Jodi was forced to start a brand-new life, feeling hopeless and lonely, miserable and sad. She'd dodged a life of foster care by hitting the streets. Truth was the streets seemed safer. She had wide-open spaces to run from the pedophiles who posed squeaky clean on the child protective services paperwork.

Shaking off the depressing memories of her past, Jodi led the way into the crowded foyer of Arcadia. The entertainment complex, situated at the heart of the West End theater district, comprised several luxurious function rooms and cinemas, the perfect setting for this glittering occasion. Carlotta progressed through the throng like royalty, stopping from time to time to share a word or an air kiss with the lucky few.

They climbed a flight of carpeted steps to enter the lavishly decorated reception room where they were to dine before the private showing of *Ultimate Betrayal*, Carlotta's new film, which many in the know tipped as a possible Oscar nominee. Deep red curtains hung from every wall swagged over television screens showing brief clips from the movie and shots of the stars discussing their roles. Jodi led Carlotta to their appointed table right in the center and held out her chair.

Carlotta waved away the offered champagne, ignoring the waiter. "Jodi, darling," she cooed, "would you mind getting me a large gin and tonic? I can't abide this weak fizzy stuff."

Well used to Carlotta's idiosyncrasies, Jodi patted her hand and smiled at the wine waiter assigned to their table. "Could you rustle up a triple gin and tonic, please?"

Carlotta gave her a nod as the waiter scurried off to carry out the starlet's wishes.

Jodi took in the scene. Everyone was exchanging light cheek kisses, hugs, and handshakes. She noticed how young most of the women looked, some barely in their thirties. Jodi shifted uneasily in her chair. Her fortieth birthday was right around the corner, two weeks, to be exact. She'd finally given in to Amelia's pleas to have a gathering of friends and call it a party. There weren't many people she could call her friend. Being regularly torn from homes she'd barely gotten comfy in kept her from connecting with others, a trait she'd carried even into her adult life. Her chosen career didn't help. She didn't need the raised eyebrows and whispers behind her back. What she did with her time was no concern to anyone else. Over the years, she'd learned to keep people at a distance. It was safer that way.

A young woman wearing an elegant black dress with large diamond studs winking from her earlobes passed in front of Jodi. There wasn't a wrinkle on her flawless skin, not even a faint laughter line around her soft blue eyes. Jodi watched her long after she'd rejoined her group of friends.

Why did youth suddenly bother her? Sure, she was getting older, but she was escorting one of the wealthiest women in the room. Carlotta didn't seem to mind that Jodi had several years on these women, almost twenty in some cases. Was it her style and personality that kept Carlotta and others just like her requesting her services? Or was it the extra personal care she gave them come night's end? She sure as hell hadn't come this far by simply shaking hands.

The question nagged at her, confused her.

She'd never had to worry about her looks.

Why all of a sudden did it matter?

Eve rushed along the sidewalk toward her office, skillfully dodging the slower New Yorkers. Late. As usual. Somehow, she was always faster than everyone else, even with the heels of her worn favorite black spiked boots punctuating her tardiness. The poor boots had seen much better days; once thick leather was now so pliable she feared ripping them every time she pulled them on. Yet she couldn't bring herself to toss them away. They were finally broken in, dammit.

She loosened her scarf, took a sip of Starbucks coffee, and then ripped open a nutrition bar with her teeth.

Her Bluetooth chirped. She bumped the button with the heel of her hand.

"I don't want bad news, Khandi. I'm having a nonviolent walk this morning. Only one bitch has given me the stink eye when I shoved around her slow ass." Eve darted around a woman leading an ankle-biter on a leash and got her second glare of the morning. "Okay, make that two."

"Roger is freaking out. He's already called this morning cussing about some last-minute change you made in the schedule. Next thing I knew he was laughing like some crazed fool, then he called me names, Eve. Ugly names. He's evil."

Eve smiled. Some people tagged her personal assistant and only friend an airhead. Eve considered her to be entertainment in her otherwise hectic life. There wasn't a dull moment in her presence. She dodged yet another slow walker. "He does not hate you, Khandi. He's just ornery sometimes."

"He called me a lint licker."

Eve coughed and managed not to spew a mouthful of coffee on the businessman traveling about the same speed beside her. "A what?"

"A lint licker. He called me a damn lint licker. What the hell does that even mean?"

"You must have misunderstood him."

"I most certainly did not misunderstand him. And don't play all angelic on me. You know he's evil. That's why you hired him. To fuck with me and make my life miserable."

"Yep, you caught me. Totally busted. I only hired the best organizer money could buy to make your day a living hell." Eve stopped at the intersection and waited for the walk sign. "Are you done exaggerating or was there more news for me?"

"You have a conference call with Shanigan's at ten sharp, about the new material you ordered. The samples arrived by courier thirty minutes ago. They're on your desk. Your meeting with Angelica at eleven is still on. She has some new models for you to look over, and your lunch with Oliver has been bumped up to twelve to go over the travel arrangements." Khandi took a deep breath. "And Francesca expects a call from you about one of the designs sometime today. I'll be sure to have Roger on line for you as soon as you walk through the doors."

"Aren't you the sweetest?"

"Bite me."

Eve laughed and disconnected the call. Day after day, same setup, same rushed life. Some would have buckled under the stress long before now, but not Eve. She was born to be a get-up-and-go girl, always hustling and always on top of every matter. She couldn't operate any other way, and her career thrived for that very reason.

Even her employees catered to her every whim. If they couldn't stop, drop, and roll when she snapped her fingers, she had no use for them. That lack of dedication only meant they were in the wrong line of work. If they had sniffling toddlers at home that needed mommy's attention, then home was where she sent them, usually for good. She needed fast-paced people and accepted nothing less. Khandi seemed the only exception to that rule; Eve sometimes needed Khandi's dizzy-headed drama to break up the rigidity of her life.

Today, her anxiety was at a peak. She needed to square away the final plans for the London trip, the finishing plot for fashion week. The event loomed large on the horizon, followed close by Milan and Paris. She needed to snap the final puzzle pieces together before she watched her creations sway down the catwalk. This wasn't her first fashion show, but it still made her giddy to see her designs evolve into reality, to watch the sales soar. She couldn't let her guard down this close to show time. Overwhelmed at times, she welcomed the rushed high these events provided.

Eve crossed the busy street and her mind whipped to Lexi, to their phone sex the previous night. Her body was splendidly sore, still tingled in the most sensitive places. Lexi knew how to make a girl feel whole, fulfilled, and utterly satisfied.

She often wondered if Lexi was her real name, though she was positive a sex operator would never use her given name. Why on earth would she? Did she truly have unkempt hair that drove Eve crazy to run her fingers through, or that lickable six-pack tummy Eve dreamed of biting, then licking away the sting? Or those dreamy green eyes into which she could fall, even drown? Eve was positive she'd let those private descriptions of her fantasy woman slip out during one phone call or another and Lexi used them to ratchet up the sexual tension. Eve smirked at her silliness. Of course, she wasn't any of those wonderful things. But it sure beat the probable truth—that Lexi was some six-hundred-pound slob who spent her time devouring Ding Dongs and cutting her toenails while Eve came apart panting her name.

She shuddered at the thought. As many times as she'd asked herself why the hell she continued the phone sex, there was only one answer. Because Lexi's voice was volcanic and made her succumb to her wicked dominance, made her lose control willingly with the mere whisper of her name. Dammit, it was the only sexual outing she had time for and a hell of a lot safer than reliving dead-end relationships. She just wasn't meant to have a partner in life, and she was okay with that.

She and Lexi lived worlds apart. She'd never have the chance to prove her theory correct, nor did she have any inclination to. Even the thought of being in the same country, in the very same city, Eve still didn't wish to meet her. She had the perfect elusive fantasy every time she dialed that memorized number. Besides, if the world didn't know she'd had phone sex with a beached whale, she'd know, and that was harmful enough.

As promised, Khandi had Roger waiting on the phone when Eve stepped into the office. She looped her scarf and coat on the rack by the front door while Khandi grinned. Today Khandi wore a tight black skirt and frilly silk blouse, and that smirk only added a luminous glow to her shiny lip gloss.

"Line one," she cooed from her perch behind the computer.

Eve blew her a kiss and disappeared into the office.

She dropped into the desk chair and answered the call. "Hi, Roger. I hear you're having problems this morning?"

"We had a discrepancy with two interviews in London but I've taken care of it."

"I have no doubts you take very good care of my schedule."

"I do try."

"Khandi mentioned there was a, um, misunderstanding during your conversation?"

"Oh, is that what she called it?" Roger laughed, a sound Eve rarely heard from him. "I call it watching a funny Orbit commercial and talking out loud."

Eve giggled with him and looked up to find Khandi draped in the doorframe, her long brown straight hair tucked behind one ear, her brow raised questioningly. "Not in so many words. I'll be sure to have a word with her."

"Great. Now get to work. Chat later."

Eve disconnected the call and turned her attention to e-mails, knowing her silence would torture Khandi. "Could you get me the full body shots of the latest models? Oh, and get Roger back on the line for me. I ditched the old prop crew after the fiasco last year and he's recommended someone out of London. I almost forgot that I need to chat with him about her work before I decide to hire her for the London show."

"Is that all?"

"No. Bring me the sketches for Milan and Paris. I'm not happy with one of the gowns. Thinking about switching a few."

"And?"

Eve studied her over the monitor, fighting back the trapped grin. "A cup of coffee?"

Eve smiled. God, she loved her life. The perfect career with all the bumps and bruises, a perfect assistant to torture and tease, the very one who kept Eve on her toes and doubled over with laughter, and the perfect sex life with a woman she'd never have to kick out of her bed.

Life couldn't get any more perfect than that.

Chapter Three

Jodi eyed the short woman heading her way. Despite a pleasant smile and a sparkle in her blue eyes, something in the attendant's manner had Jodi squeezing the arms of the spa chair. It wasn't the sexy twist of hips that had Jodi on the verge of racing from the room; it was the bowl in her grasp. The heap of green gloop resembled guacamole, and though it would be a tasty treat, she knew the concoction wasn't edible. Jodi mentally came up with a thousand excuses why she shouldn't stay seated any longer as the woman came to an easy stop beside her.

Jodi raised a brow as the woman placed the bowl on the table and gave her a nod. "Hi. My name's Rachel. I'll be your esthetician today. We're going to start with a thorough cleansing followed by a skin analysis to determine what exfoliations we'll be using on you. You ready to begin?"

The technician might as well have spoken Greek for all the sense she made. Jodi stared dumbfounded. With or without Amelia giggling beside her, what madness had possessed her to step foot inside a damn girly spa?

Amelia's giggles turned into laughter. "It's mud, chickenshit. It's for your foot massage. It takes away all the nasty dead skin." She patted Jodi's hand as if that would ease the chill of being out of her element. "It's not poison. I promise."

Normally, Jodi wouldn't have given in to Amelia's pleas to spend the day getting shit caked on her face or an emery board swiped under her nails or, God forbid, someone touching her feet, but last night's date, surrounded by women who wouldn't see crow's feet for years, made her think twice about Amelia's invitation.

Jodi kept her gaze trained on the petite beautician, who removed plastic sticks from the drawer as carefully as a dental assistant setting up for oral surgery.

Amelia cackled. "The expression on your face is priceless. Damn, where's my Kodak when I need it?"

Jodi kept a wary eye on the contents. "Shut up, Amelia."

"All right, sourpuss, do tell. What pushed my butch best friend into the throes of the dreaded day spa?" Amelia lay back while her own attendant cleansed her face with a long cotton pad. Jodi's beautician squirted something toxic onto a cotton ball. "Did someone point out the permanent wrinkle between your eyes?"

Jodi studied Amelia, how her body lounged and relaxed as her aide expertly circled the pad. "First off, I don't have a permanent anything between my eyes, thank you very much. Second, even if I did, no one would be brave enough to point it out." Despite her vehement denial, she self-consciously rubbed the indention between her eyes.

"Oooh. Aren't you the tough dyke? And what's wrong with growing old gracefully?" Amelia chuckled as Jodi's attendant stepped beside the chair and motioned for her to lie back.

Jodi ignored Amelia's question as she tried to get comfy, mainly because graceful didn't have anything to do with the age spots appearing along the edge of her hairline. Not only was she growing old, she was aging alone. She might have Amelia, but she couldn't curl up with her best friend on rainy days, couldn't wake in a tangle of arms and legs after a sleepless night of making love.

So where was her soul mate? Where was that person who would love her unconditionally? Had she passed Jodi by while she had a client spread out like a feast, while she fattened her savings?

The esthetician touched Jodi's face with something soft. Jodi jerked back and gave the woman a hard look. "Is this going to peel off the top five layers of my face? Will I be beet red for a year?"

"No, darling, it's just a cleanser. We wouldn't dream of peeling your face off until it's squeaky clean." A mischievous grin broke across her lips while Amelia and her attendant laughed.

Jodi had no choice but to laugh along, the act relaxing her otherwise jammed nerves. "Ha ha, funny." She attempted to set her breathing back to normal.

"There you go. Just relax." She placed a hair band around Jodi's head that instantly made her feel constricted. And feminine. This shit was for girls, not tough butches.

She closed her eyes just as Amelia snickered. "Don't you look cute with that pretty purple band in your hair?"

Jodi lifted her hand and shot her a bird while her mind screamed to jerk the damn thing off her scalp. Too afraid she'd fall into Amelia's plot, she stilled the impulse as the attendant's thigh brushed her arm. Her nipples peaked in instant awareness. A feminine body always had a way of calming her. She resisted opening her eyes to see if the action had been deliberate.

"Are you asking me to sit and spin on that finger of yours?" Amelia purred in her mocking Cinderella tone. "Got something a little bigger?"

"Yeah, my fist, for that mouth." The aide continued working the cotton pad across Jodi's face. She laid her arm back on the rest as those thighs pressed harder against her upper arm. Deliberate indeed. Heat flooded her crotch. Maybe this trip to the spa wouldn't turn out so bad after all.

"I know somewhere else you can put it," Amelia teased. Fact was, Amelia was straight as a stick. Though they'd shared desk space to tease and torture their phone customers all those years ago, it was deep throats and ball-massaging techniques Amelia had described to her male clients. Just as Amelia tuned in to guys, Jodi had known her sexuality from the second little Emily Peterson had shared her chocolate milk at recess on the military base in South Carolina. Girls were far easier to play with. Guys were just rough jerks. It didn't take her too many years to figure out girls smelled delicious and tasted just as enticing.

"You couldn't handle me. I'd put your boy toys to shame."

"Pussy."

"I'm gonna show you pussy."

"Hold that image for your birthday party. Lordy, Lordy, Jodi's forty. You old ass," she said with an evil laugh.

Jodi huffed. Leave it to Amelia to slap the reality on with a trowel. "Keep it up over there, Ms. Forty-two. And change the subject, for shit's sake."

"Ooh, did I tickle your clit the wrong way?"

Both attendants snickered.

Fact was her clit wasn't getting tickled, flicked, sucked, or even massaged by anyone other than herself. She didn't allow herself two-way satisfaction and definitely didn't exchange delicate kisses, not even in heated passion. Such acts were for personal dates only. Maybe that's what she needed—a good fuck to flush out the new obsession with her looks. Since when did she start caring about her appearance or how many wrinkles she had? She looked good, and she knew it. Four to five times a week she worked out until sweat gleamed off her well-deserved six-pack. Okay, so she only exerted herself for all the women ogling from their treadmills, but that didn't change the outcome. She was in damn good shape and had looks to complete the package. Her fat bank account only proved the theory. She had steady "dates," ones who always came back for more. Obviously, they didn't care about that damn frown line snaking along her forehead, or those faint laugh lines spreading around her temples like crevices, the ones that grew deeper with every passing year.

"Let's talk about your good news and lay off my aging skin." Jodi switched gears, determined to get her mind off her dreaded birthday. She'd been determined to fight old age all the way to the grave. Little did she know it would involve mudpacks and toxic cleansers.

"I just signed a temporary contract with one of the hottest designers the fashion world has ever seen."

"No fucking way." Jodi practically jerked to a sitting position, but a soft hand pressed her back down. Maybe that same hand could press her thighs apart later tonight, make her forget her clock was ticking faster by the day. "With whom?"

"Don't get your briefs in a wad. Some hard-ass bitch out of New York City, who, rumor has it, is almost impossible to work for. I've heard all about her. She just fired my biggest competitor. She leaves no room for flaws, and that alone makes me nervous enough to fuck up everything. I almost backed out after my brutal and nerve-racking conference call with her yesterday, then I thought of all that lovely money and the vacations I can spend it on if I can snag a permanent spot in her events."

"No sweat. You got this bitch in the bag. Your work's impeccable." Jodi didn't like the concern in Amelia's voice. She was protective and didn't like when Amelia put herself down, especially when she'd worked so damn hard to make an honest woman of herself. She hadn't seen her get so nervous in a long time. This high-rolling New Yorker must be some kind of anal perfectionist to make Amelia that worried. "She'll be honored to have your props on her set."

"Aww. You're sweet and I love you, which is why you're going to be my sidekick."

"What?" This time Jodi came to a full sitting position, almost knocking the astringent-soaked pad from the beautician's grasp. "No, but hell no! I refuse to let you drag me into a world of outrageously self-obsessed designers who have no grounding in the real world. The models gross me out. They're like walking skeletons. Who'd want to fuck something so fragile? I'd break them." Jodi gave a low growl. She'd clawed her way through hell to keep meat on her bones. She couldn't fathom anyone starving herself to sashay down a catwalk for some fashion mongrel. "Not to mention I don't know a damn thing about designing props."

Amelia remained comfy and serene, never even opened her eyes. "Who said anything about you designing anything or fucking a so-called pencil stick model? I don't need your brain, sweetie. I just need those biceps."

Once again, the attendants snorted.

Jodi eyed her own aide and slowly lay back down. "You're supposed to be on my side here, not hers. That giggle's coming out of your tip." Jodi winked playfully before she closed her eyes and gave in to the woman's soft caresses. A thigh brushed her arm again. Jodi cracked an eye open and found the woman's expression all business as she worked the pad against her flesh.

Okay, so she wouldn't have a date tonight. Or a well-needed fuck. But soon. Soon she was going to need sexual relief. If only to take her mind off the loneliness.

"You ready for that Brazilian wax now? It won't hurt a bit. I promise," Rachel teased her.

Amelia spewed while Jodi scowled and held her hand protectively over her crotch. "I'll pass, thanks."

❖

Eve shifted in her seat. She hated flying. Not to mention a seven-hour flight across the Atlantic. She was always convinced her day was marked while over the choppy waters down below. Flying was a necessity to her career, so she reined in her fear every flight and said a silent prayer the plane would implode on impact, that she'd never know what hit her.

Khandi hummed to her iPod beside her, sometimes singing out loud, which had people turning around to give dirty looks. Eve thought about poking her to end the torture but knew she would only deliberately sing louder and more out of tune. God forbid.

To take her mind off the turbulence, Eve opened her laptop and studied the twelve sketches she'd chosen for the London event. Her stomach knotted with excitement as she studied the creations. Her creations. The final breathtaking product awaited her in London, along with her beloved seamstress. Francesca had been a doll all these years, putting up with Eve's last-minute changes, sometimes expecting them, yet rarely complaining.

When work couldn't hold Eve's attention, she put the computer away and closed her eyes. She allowed Lexi's image to blossom in her mind. It was after a rough day like today, when problems seemed to pop up out of nowhere, especially when her fear was spiked to the limits over salty waters, that she sought Lexi's attention, her voice, and her commands. Knowing what those seductive demands could bring her made her ache for the sound of Lexi all the more.

Eve instinctively reached for her cell phone, then remembered she was flying far above the Atlantic. "Shit." She huffed, needing that sexy accent to take her away.

Khandi shifted and nudged Eve. The smartass pointed to the flight phone with a knowing sarcastic grin.

Eve rolled her eyes. The bitch. Why, again, had she shared her secret with Khandi? That she phoned a woman halfway across the world several times a week just to melt in her sexy voice, to follow her commands, to come screaming by her orders? She knew she could trust Khandi with her personal business, always had been able to, but the fact that Khandi could tease and torture her with her own weakness, and did as often as possible, was something she hadn't thought through before she'd blurted out her secret.

Khandi pushed the ear buds back in and started rocking her head, gradually kicking up the volume of her voice. A woman in the seat in front of them turned around to glare again, her lips set tight and an ugly frown line creased on her forehead. Khandi waved and gave her an angelic smile, then continued singing, as if someone else was the intended target of the woman's glare.

Eve blew out a breath and turned toward the window, to the clouds and water below. With every passing minute she was getting closer to that other side of the world, where "her" Lexi lived, walked, and worked daily, doing only God knew what. Eve was going to be inside her city, possibly passing her on the streets without being the wiser. Would she be as sexy as her mind had conjured? Or would she be as grotesque as her evil twin had predicted? It was a fact she'd never know. She couldn't handle being the brunt of Khandi's mockery, or her own for that matter, if she were to come face-to-face with that proof.

Eve tapped her fingers on the arm of the chair.

Khandi giggled and Eve turned an impatient stare on her. "Here, do it. You know you want to. I'll even crank my music louder so you can have your privacy. Oh, Lexi! Oh, Lexiiiii." Khandi threw her head back, her lips parted in fake ecstasy.

Eve slapped her hand over Khandi's mouth, controlling the impulse to wrap the headphone cords around her neck to see how pretty blue oxygen-deprived lips would match her shit brown eyes.

"You're pushing it, lint licker." Eve removed her hand and pushed the phone away while Khandi broke into laughter. A man dressed in a deep gray business suit turned from his laptop and gave them a "shut the fuck up" scowl. Khandi waved at him too.

Eve eased higher in her seat and looked down the aisle for the flight attendant. A drink was what she needed, anything to take away the constant throb in her crotch. Was this addiction? This gnawing need rooted so deep in her consciousness. In her pussy. She could take care of her own sexual frustrations. Had done it for many years. She didn't need Lexi, or her voice, to extinguish the burning sensations. So why was Lexi the one she sought? Why was Lexi's voice the one she craved?

"Here. If you're going to be a dud with the phone, at least read some London gossip." Khandi tossed a magazine in her lap. "Maybe the hottie escorting Ms. Carlotta Tate down the red carpet will ease your…needs. Rumor has it she's an escort, like a real paid, fuck 'em for my paycheck escort."

Without looking, Eve pushed the tabloid away. She didn't give a shit who did what in London. Right now, all she cared about was getting some alone time with her cell phone and that voice that seduced her into submission.

❖

Jodi ran the feather duster over the bookcase shelves, then turned to the coffee table while Erica moaned into the phone.

"That's it. Fuck yourself harder, faster." Jodi finished dusting the table and began on the flat screen TV set against the outer living room wall of windows. Night flickered beyond the glass.

She stopped to look out over the bright white lights while Erica panted heavily. Every room in the condo held a panoramic view of the vast city below with floor-to-ceiling and wall-to-wall windows. It was the feature that had sold her on the apartment. Hell, it was the deciding factor when she opted to buy the whole building.

The openness made her feel free and never constricted.

"Lexi. God, it feels so good."

Jodi moved away from the window with the sound of her name. The living room stretched to the right and left, a cream-colored extra-long couch dominating the opposite wall. Matching artsy scoop-back chairs dotted the corners and either side of the entertainment center. The only color in the room was from the jade green pillows scattered on the couch.

The room looked clean. Made her feel clean.

"Lexi, I'm coming!" Erica's moans erupted down the line.

Jodi blinked, reminded she was on the phone.

"Yes, come, Erica. Come hard."

"Oh God, I am. Coming so damn hard."

Jodi walked barefoot into the kitchen and put the duster in the cupboard. "Pump, baby. Drive that vibrator deeper." She selected a sparkling water from the fridge, then went back through the living room and onto the balcony that ran the length of her apartment.

After curling up in a chair, she uncapped the bottle and drank until it was half-empty.

Erica hummed in satisfaction. "I'm drained."

"Good. Now pull those sheets over your naked body, close your eyes, and go to sleep, my sweet."

"Night, Lexi."

"Night, Erica."

Jodi disconnected the call and leaned back to look out over the river. The skyscrapers doubled in the reflection, masking the water in pinks and purples.

She couldn't imagine living anywhere else. This felt like home—this apartment, this river, this city. It'd taken years to bond with the surroundings, with this country, but now that she had, she never wanted to be anywhere else. She frequently blessed her mother for registering her birth in both the USA and the United Kingdom, thus giving her the freedom to choose her place of residence by virtue of dual nationality. One day, she'd venture out and be free to explore all the places the military had never given her time to see.

The clock in the art district chimed the midnight hour. It was late afternoon on Eve's side of the world. Although, knowing Eve, she was probably still working, going about in her rushed career, whatever that might be.

But soon, she'd call. She'd need Lexi to bring her back down from her high, would need Lexi to strip away her power, to make her come.

Jodi sighed, smiled, and took another drink.

CHAPTER FOUR

Eve fanned photos across the table in her suite and studied each model, looking for a certain shape for each gown. She was also checking their body language and the aura of confidence in them that told her they'd show off her design like a masterpiece. But most of all, she was looking for meat. Nothing aggravated her more than a model displaying a cage of ribs. She'd witnessed malnutrition more times than she cared to share and absolutely refused to hire a model who craved fame more than her own health. There would never be a size zero walking in her fashion show.

Angelica, the owner of the talent agency Eve had been contracting with for the past seven years, sat beside her. The black business slacks and deep purple jacket rimmed with a wisp of fringe proclaimed the sort of self-assurance Eve looked for in her associates. Her shoulder-length brown hair swung along her cheek as she reached out. "These are the new models I just acquired." She pulled three particular shots closer to Eve. "Theresa has striking poses and a self-assured walk that's completely natural, while the other two are a bit timid and unsure of themselves. Still getting their feet wet. I have faith all three won't let you down. They've been working very hard."

"I trust your judgment. Have them meet us at the studio for a walk-through. Get with Khandi for the schedule." Eve felt underdressed in her slouchy loose jeans and a worn Yankees T-shirt. She'd shed her business attire as soon as she entered the suite, needing a shower to erase the heat from thoughts of someone's sexy voice. Or the lack of it.

"Certainly." Angelica plucked up her BlackBerry and eased away from the table.

Eve continued matching models to the sketches. The final decisions would come when the models went through the pre-walk rehearsal, when Eve would have a better view of what the pictures couldn't capture—their coolness and aplomb plus the way they would portray each of her designs. She actually hated that part, having to wave away a model who didn't make the cut, someone who'd worked hard to earn a spot on her runway. Not all made it, and as much as it saddened her to break their hearts, only the strong survived in her world and she never hesitated to dismiss anyone, tears and all.

Trying to block out the noise and bustle around her, Eve slid the possible matches to the side. The show was on the road as more people filed into the large room for their kick-off business meeting. Some she didn't even know; some she didn't need to know. She usually enjoyed this point in the process, yet today it irked her. Conversations merged together, making the room loud with unintelligible chatter.

Lexi was the reason for her distraction. Or rather, what Lexi could give her. Complete surrender. She needed a Lexi fix to swipe away the tension twisting her insides into a tightly coiled knot, to get back on track. Only then could she give one hundred percent of her mind to work.

Thankfully, Khandi had whisked Roger to the couch to go over their weeklong hectic schedule. Eve didn't know what she'd do without handy Khandi sometimes. She took care of the less pressing arrangements that would only bog Eve down.

The hair and makeup artists stood in the corner, their laughter a bit too loud and their stories way too erotic as they exchanged details of their previous night on the town. The men they'd taken to their beds. Their conversation made her think even more of Lexi. Made her wonder who Lexi took to her bed, who she fucked. The thought made her gut rumble.

Hungry. She was hungry. She pushed out of her chair and found herself looking into Francesca's smiling black eyes.

"Oh my God!" Eve's spirits lifted immediately as she crushed her in her arms. Francesca was a woman who could work miracles with fabric less than the length of a handkerchief. "It's so fucking great to see you. You're like a breath of fresh air in this noisy room."

"Are you having a bad day?" Francesca pulled back slightly. "I brought you something to cheer you up." She nodded toward the door leading to Eve's bedroom where a temporary hook attached to the frame held extra garments.

The air caught in Eve's lungs as she found the black and crimson gown that had caused her complete misery from the second its image had scurried through her mind. No matter how many ways she'd drawn her vision, she couldn't define the elegant lines of her dream gown. A sucker for a challenge, she'd sketched and re-sketched, arguing with Francesca every step of the way, Francesca claiming the material would not hold the lustrous look Eve desired, that too much fabric would have to be cut away to open the sides while leaving enough coverage across the breasts. After months of Francesca proving her point with endless photos of her progress, Eve had thrown up her hands and dismissed the design altogether, though she had to admit it had lingered in the darkest recesses of her mind, always poking like a stiff finger.

Yet here it hung—long, luminous black shimmering silk. Running from one hip to an opposite shoulder, curving in to expose a model's lean tummy, another curve forming an S to wrap like a lover's hand around breasts, an elegant twist of material shimmered with red metal flake. The gown was backless, held together by a single delicate rose-shaped knot at the neck.

Eve stood transfixed by its elegance.

"You like?"

"How did…it's…it's my vision exactly. Like you plucked it right out of my head." Eve looked from Francesca to the gown, then finally moved from her frozen spot.

She approached the gown as if it were alive, as if the mere invasion of its space might make it flee. Finally, she reached out to touch the miraculous creation, the material soft as baby powder against her fingers. "It's breathtaking."

"Eve, how many models did you decide on?" Angelica's voice interrupted Eve's fascination.

"We have a discrepancy in our timeline for tomorrow, Eve. Roger is turning a few ugly shades of blue and green over here. He's going to hyperventilate if we don't go over the schedule, and I don't know CPR," Khandi yelled from somewhere behind her.

"Ms. Harris." Sandra, the makeup artist who'd been in deep

conversation about sex only a few minutes ago, claimed her attention, aggravation etched in her voice. "It was our understanding there would be twelve models for the show. We may need another artist if there will be more than that."

Once again, voices rose above each other, throwing anxious questions her way; cell phones chirped and sang, all while Eve was held captivated by the prize. Her hectic life, the rushed way in which she spent almost every waking moment of her days; the reason was staring back at her. Everything culminated in this gripping emotional finish. It all came down to the very thing she was staring at—her creations breathing life.

Business awaited. Eve sighed, dragged her gaze away from the gown, and turned back to Francesca. "Duty calls, my love. You have brightened my day, for sure. Thank you so much." Eve gave her another hug, then turned back to the eager faces waiting to jerk her back into the throng of work.

"You work too much. It will be your death if you don't take a break." Francesca patted Eve's shoulder. "I will see you at the theater. Everything's going to be fine." She removed the dress from the hook and headed through the chaotic frenzy of people.

Eve's stomach rumbled, reminding her she'd been en route to the snack bar set up against the far wall before Francesca's stunning creation sidetracked her. She scooted around a tight-knit group she assumed to be the lighting crew since she caught the words *watts* and *voltage*, and snapped up a nutrition bar.

The chatter faded as she tore the wrapper away. Lexi came to mind instantly. She recalled Lexi making fun of her, telling her she was going to turn into an energy bar from the amount she ate. Her body heated with the memory, her insides coiling tight. Eve snuck a peek at the adjacent bedroom, at the privacy beyond the heavy oak door. If only she could slip away for five minutes, maybe ten, depending on how giving and altruistic Lexi would be in Eve's state of turmoil. This wouldn't be the first time she'd dialed that number in haste and desperation. Sometimes Lexi took her out of her misery with brunt commands and vivid images. Other times she teased Eve into a frenzy before she allowed her release. Which would she be today?

Worse, the thought of haste only brought back one of their more recent conversations, where Lexi had told Eve she'd fuck her in haste.

Her clit pulsed.

Eve snapped around to the faces in the room in hopes of forcing her mind to forget that her crotch was heating, that she needed some relief before she dove back into the battle zone. Francesca was ducking out the suite door with the dress held protectively against her chest, almost daring anyone to come near her. Eve had to laugh, considering Francesca barely came to the shoulders of the shortest person in the room. Across the room, Roger was tapping his pen impatiently on his crossed leg, a sure sign his timeline was being stretched to the limit. Angelica was looking over the photos, her BlackBerry snug against her ear. Finally, Eve looked to the window. It was raining. She didn't remember the rain in London being quite so pretty, or blue.

She wished she could perform magic and make everyone in the room vanish in a puff of smoke so she could dial Lexi's number. She needed to hear Lexi's voice, needed her sanity stripped for a few glorious minutes, for one fucking orgasm. God save her soul, but she didn't know why. Sex was sex, and this wasn't ordinary sex. For crying out loud, she had phone sex with a woman who could look like Attila the Hun for all she knew, or worse, might be as old as her mother.

The thought sent a chill down her spine, and she quickly bit into the dry grains of oats, fruit, and peanut butter to ease the pang of discomfort eating at her.

She took a deep breath and headed toward Khandi. Roger would burst at the seams if she didn't attempt to right the wrong in the agenda. Anal was an understatement when it came to Roger and a schedule. He'd lift hell and drop it in the Bermuda Triangle to stay on target. It was the very reason she'd hired him.

Khandi looked up. She gave Eve an evil smile, then mouthed, "You have service now."

The bitch! Eve made a mental note to seek revenge as soon as they were through with this circus. She bit off another chunk and headed back into the fire pit of business. Her life.

❖

Jodi couldn't stop the tug at her crotch when the phone rang and she recognized Eve's number in the ID window.

She noted the time. So early? Eve must be having a horrible

beginning to her day. And she hadn't called last night. Jodi had fallen asleep in the balcony chair with the light breeze drifting across her face, phone in her lap, and awoken several hours later. This wasn't the first time Eve hadn't called, but lately, the calls had become more frequent.

Normally, Eve's calls came at the day's end, when her frustration peaked, sometimes when "Lexi" was deep in sleep. As much as she hated having her beauty rest interrupted, Jodi always made an exception for Eve. Welcomed it, in fact.

Something must have set her off today, or maybe she'd taken a day off. Jodi almost chuckled at the thought. Her little work maniac would never dream of something so out of character. Jodi might not know much about the woman who set her crotch on fire with a whimper, but she knew her work habits like clockwork. She couldn't wait to hear those cries of self-satisfaction. Giving Eve release was always her pleasure, no matter what time of day it was in either of their worlds.

Jodi kicked in the British accent she only used for phone sex and pressed the Talk button. She never expected to meet a client, but she'd seen far crazier things in her life. Besides, this accent was far sexier than a Texas country twang. "Good morning, my early bird. Who would dream of upsetting you with barely a start to your day?"

The pause on the line made Jodi check to see if she'd connected.

"Oh, yes…it's morning," Eve said, her low murmur turning swiftly into a soft laugh. "It's chaotic here. I just needed a few minutes to myself."

Jodi snuggled deeper in the chaise against the window where she'd been lounging with an old novel. She tossed the book to the side. Eve needed her.

"What are you wearing, Eve?" Jodi could hear the unspoken truth, the "I need you" laced in her words. It pleased her that Eve thought of her, wanted her, even if it was only her voice. Today, she would show mercy. She would take Eve quickly. "Don't tell me. Just take it off."

Jodi often wished she knew what Eve did for a living, the career that kept her swarmed and uptight so often. She wanted to picture what her day must truly be like. Was she a nurse? No, nurses didn't work as much as Eve did. But doctors did. No, she didn't strike her as a doctor. Too fast. A lawyer? Surely not. Too mouthy for a judge, though Jodi could well imagine she'd give an offending attorney a run for his money.

What did she look like? Did she have long hair? That thought always drove Jodi crazy. She wanted to sift Eve's locks through her fingers, to tug the strands into her fist as she pumped deep. Was she slim and fit? Was she as gorgeous as her voice projected?

No attachments, share nothing personal, keep the sex business. It keeps them coming back. Rona's words rang in her mind. She'd died three years ago, but the lessons she'd taught Jodi had carried her far in this so-called business, had indeed taught her how to keep her schedule full and her bank account fat. Jodi had absorbed her sessions like a sponge, wanting more than the phone clients, wanting more than the needy women seeking relief. The women she "dated" sought the same thing, but she shined in their world. She was their mysterious adventuress, the quench to their secluded sex thirst.

Though she'd tried to leave the sex operator life far behind, two clients had stood out from the pack. Both still called at least once a week. Then Eve had called one day out of the blue. She never had learned where Eve had acquired her private line, nor did she care. Somehow, Eve had found her way to Jodi, to Lexi, and she was happy to provide what Eve craved—more than happy, in fact.

"I'm naked now. And wet."

"Pinch your nipples. I want them rosy red and stiff peaks. Don't stop until the pain is like fire between your thighs."

"Jesus!" Eve panted.

"Make it burn, Eve."

"It does burn. It always burns so hot. Fuck me, Lexi."

"You're too easy, my sex fiend." Jodi clenched her insides, her pussy already tingling with Eve's heavy breathing. As much as she wanted to touch herself, she couldn't. It was her law, the unbridled rule that kept her sane. "Now, I need to you to follow my instructions, Eve. Can you do that?"

"Yes, please. Hurry. I need to come, Lexi."

"Place your fingers against those wet lips, and then gently press down until your clit slides up and through."

"I don't under…oh, God."

"Have you exposed that little pink hood?"

"Yes, shit, yes. Help me, Lexi."

"With your other hand, caress the tip. Be gentle. It's very sensitive."

"Fuck! Oh, fuck. It stings so good. Like pain. Like pleasure. I need to come, Lexi. So bad."

"You will, my impatient Eve. You will." Jodi angled in her chair to see the river better. Rain twisted down the window like shimmering lines of silver. As long as she could focus on the droplets, she could fight off the urges Eve awakened inside her. "Drive those fingers inside yourself. Push deep, Eve."

Jodi focused straight ahead when Eve mewed, winging the sound to the back of her mind as fast as it had spilled from Eve's lips. The line between composure and losing control was thin, always too thin.

"I'm fucking myself, Lexi."

"Yes, you are, my pet. Fuck yourself. Listen to my voice, push deeper; squeeze your fingers around that clit."

"I can't control myself," Eve whispered. "I'm coming, Lexi."

Eve's soft cries poured down the line and Jodi closed her eyes, fierce clenches ripping at her insides. With her jaw gripped tight, she shoved back in the chair and squeezed her hands into fists.

She was scared. Eve scared her. Or rather, her uncontrolled reaction terrified her. Hundreds of women had come screaming with her name falling from their lips, by Lexi's voice. Maybe just as many had come pumping beneath her, by Jodi's hands. Not a single one had the power to steal her grip on her control like Eve did with every pant and moan and cry of pleasure.

Eve's breathing calmed while Jodi fought for discipline. Maybe she should consider dropping Eve from her tiny list of phone clients. Or finally disconnect the private line altogether. She'd been considering it for many years, never truly having a reason to, yet never having a reason not to.

"I'm pathetic. I have a room full of people. Everyone bidding for my attention."

"Sounds enticing, everyone bidding for you."

"It's not. I feel suffocated sometimes." Eve sighed. "That's not true. Not completely. Shit, I don't know what's wrong with me."

Jodi wasn't sure if she should be paying attention, yet she was like a monkey on a branch, hanging on Eve's every word, too afraid she'd miss some pivotal information to explain why her heart swayed every time she called. Every time she came.

"Are your people safe for you to return to now?"

Eve chuckled and Jodi could tell she was dressing. The fact calmed her. The fact that Eve was no longer naked, and alone, with only Jodi's—Lexi's—voice to keep her company. For as often as she talked about people, crowds, and commotion, she was alone, and Jodi could hear the loneliness too often.

"Yes, I believe so."

"Then mission accomplished."

"The rain is beautiful."

Jodi snapped her attention to the window, to the glimmering purple rain. Something clamped tight in her soul.

"But you hate the rain." Jodi tensed. Rona's warning words rang loud. *If you insist with this foolishness of keeping your sex line, let me give you a little advice. Do not let their personal confessions in the throes of passion break you. These women are lonely for a reason only they need know. Give them the pleasure they seek. Nothing more. Never let their words reach your heart.*

Too late for that. Rona was right. She'd gotten too comfortable with Eve, shared things she'd never shared with another, not even to Amelia.

"I do hate the rain. But I think I can see why you love this…I mean the rain. For some reason, today I want to get naked and run until I'm drenched and owned by it."

Jodi found herself in a trance, watching the rain sparkle like diamonds against the panes. Why had she shared that part of herself with Eve? It'd been too personal. It'd been a delicate piece of her heart that belonged only to her. Had she shared it because Eve had offered a part of herself to Jodi? To Lexi?

She fingered a small stream from inside the window, wondering if the rain smelled as fresh in New York as it did in London. Was it as potent and tranquilizing? Could it make Eve feel as cleansed as Jodi's rain did?

Jodi wasn't supposed to care. Yet she did. For some reason, she did. Not only that, she wanted to know what Eve looked like. She wanted to know if that sultry voice matched her outer beauty. She could be butt-ugly, missing a mouthful of teeth. She could be the hunchback's baby sister. Either way, Jodi wanted to know. She almost needed to know.

Rona was probably spinning in her grave.

Jodi was doing it.

She was getting attached to the client.

Chapter Five

Jodi wheeled her Lincoln Navigator into the appointed staff parking area, then followed an obvious group of models through the barriers and traffic cones. She stuffed her hands in her pockets, pretending to ignore their lame conversation about killer photo shoots, catwalk disasters, and all the grueling work it took to stay on top of the modeling tree. These kids didn't know what grueling meant. They were sheltered behind their perfect lives with Mommy and Daddy jumping at their every whim. Clueless. They were clueless to what really lurked outside their bubbled glass world.

Thankfully, she was wearing sunglasses to hide her impatience. Models were so damn boring. And thin. Well, weren't they supposed to be? She took a better inspection. Only one of the women was skeletally thin. It was grotesque, the lack of any visible meat and the lack of curve appeal. To the world, she was sure the one appeared glamorous and beautiful. To Jodi, she looked like a past. Her past.

She was surprised to see the other two actually looked normal. Not too thin. She wondered how they'd fare at the auditions or how quickly the designer would favor the rod-thin one and send the others home. God knew, the anorexic one would win the spot on the catwalk, fragile bones and all.

They also made her think of Zara, the sexy and alluring millionaire she'd escorted on several occasions to some elaborate party or ballroom gala. Zara never missed a fashion event with her tight-knit group of rich friends, and she always spent a small fortune on new designs. She was a fashion groupie, so to speak, living off Daddy's allowance, who'd never worked a day in her life. They'd shared some good times together, even better nights. She was a hellcat in bed and didn't much like Jodi's stone butch demeanor, something Jodi couldn't and wouldn't change, not even for a good fuck, and definitely not for any amount of cash.

The women entered the lobby of the theater, giggles erupting like a clarion of bells, and immediately rushed to the right and disappeared behind a door marked *Private*.

Jodi moved farther into the building, thankful she wouldn't have to listen to the quarrelsome chatter a second longer. Brick-red carpet with a gold paisley design led her to the grand foyer. An elongated brass chandelier hung dead center of the room, casting bright blue droplets against the walls and floor.

Row upon row of plush red velvet-covered chairs lined both sides of the long catwalk. Silver silk lavishly draped the entrance to the stage from ceiling to floor and then rippled down both sides of the runway to the circular podium at the end. The shimmering rivulets drew her to this focal point where the models would pause, turning to show off the designer's creations from every angle before moving back up the runway, passing the incoming model at the halfway point. Jodi wasn't alien to the fashion world. She'd escorted a client or two to such events. However, she'd never been behind the scenes or witnessed the show at the last-minute dash to perfection.

Jodi followed the noise, pushing her way around groups of people until she found what seemed to be the center of a battle zone. Shocked at the steady stream of people dashing to one station or another, Jodi pushed her sunglasses on top of her head. The only thing missing from this full-on war scene was military fatigues and tanks, dead bodies, and the stench of gunpowder. In its place were hordes of workers bellowing and barking orders, some over walkie-talkies, and each raising his voice to outdo the other.

Unsure which direction to go, Jodi scanned the room while people bumped and pushed around her as if she were in some imaginary path.

Relief overwhelmed her as she spotted Amelia, her hair pulled on the crown of her head in a messy bun, a pencil tucked over one ear, and a camera lens focused on the glamorous runway. Jodi rushed to her side like a lost toddler to a mother. She'd never seen so much controlled chaos in her life. She much preferred the after-scene, when everyone had their shit together.

"How can you think coherently in this place? I thought I'd walked into a rehearsal for a war movie." Jodi sidled next to Amelia just in time to avoid a collision with a woman barreling through the throng with a rack of clothing trailing in her wake.

"We're not working here. I just needed a visual and measurements of the runway before I started working on the props." Amelia turned, a smile fading from her lips, replaced by a chastising glare. "What the... why the hell are you wearing that billboard shit? You came here to work. This is not your sexual playground."

Jodi glanced down her body, at her long-sleeved white button-down shirt ending untucked over a pair of dark blue jeans. "You said you needed my brute strength. Nothing was mentioned about getting dirty." She leaned closer. "Everywhere is my sexual playground. You know that."

Amelia blew a blond wisp of hair from her cheek. "Don't make me get all kung fu on your ass. I can take you."

Jodi spun her phone accent into gear as she angled her head and leaned closer. "Would you tie me down and spank me too?"

Amelia snapped her hands on her hips. "Stop using that damn phone voice on me, you wannabe Brit." She started back through the crowd.

Jodi hurried to keep up. "Where are you going?"

Amelia easily dodged a group of people at the entrance and stepped out of the building. Without looking back, she walked against the wall under the awning. A few doors down, she ducked into a building and turned a glare on Jodi. "My new boss snagged this studio. We'll be working here all week. And you better behave, got it?"

"Ahhh. I forgot we had an in-living-color she-bitch in the house." Jodi scanned the crowd, thankful this place wasn't half as crowded as the last. "Please say she'll grace us with her presence so I can tell her where to stick that perfectionist ass of hers."

"Shhh!" Amelia clamped her fingers tightly around Jodi's upper arm and tugged her behind a wall of workers who seemed obsessed with something on a computer monitor. They looked like statuettes, all bent at the waist, all with fingers to cheeks in deep concentration. Jodi had the impulse to yell "boo" to see how high they'd jump. "So help me God, Jodi, if you do anything to embarrass—"

"Whoa, whoa. I'm kidding, Amelia." Jodi pulled her into a quick hug. The way her eyes bugged and her breathing hitched, she was on the verge of losing it. Jodi had never seen her react like this to pressure. Hell, Amelia was the epitome of tranquility. It was disturbing to see her on edge. "You need to chill out. You're going to do an incredible job. Like you always do."

"I...I just don't want to fuck this up. This could be the long-awaited jump start, you know?" She sighed against Jodi's chest and stepped out of the embrace.

"You're not going to fuck up. You wouldn't know how to." Jodi chucked her chin. "Okay, boss, where do I need to pump my muscles?" She rolled up her sleeves and wiggled her brow.

A smile crept across Amelia's lips, her cheeks rising to erase that worn expression.

Chatter rose behind them and Jodi turned to see a woman strutting across the carpet on very worn spiked leather boots. She sported a black thermal-type shirt tucked into a pair of faded jeans. The smudged edges of an Aerosmith winged logo reached from one shoulder to the other of her shirt, and Jodi couldn't take her eyes off the knotted white beads dangling between her breasts or the silver loop earrings hanging against her enticing tanned neck.

Jodi couldn't remember the last time she'd seen someone dressed in everyday attire that still made it look like fashion ripped right off the front page of *Vogue*. She was sexy in a fun and easy kind of way, yet she bore an expression that screamed all business. Jodi wanted to fuck her.

A flock of men and women formed a semicircle around her like she was a major celebrity. Jodi didn't have to hear the sharp intake of breath or see the look of fear in Amelia's eyes to know the woman was her new boss.

And what a delightfully yummy boss she was. Standing barely 5'4" on those pathetic excuses for boots, and her body language and rushed steps screamed power. Long raven curls bounced freely around her face and down her back and Jodi had an image of fisting the strands in her grasp while she pushed her down to her knees. She couldn't force her gaze away as the group drew closer. The woman looked from one of her following to another as they dueled impatiently for her attention.

Jodi mentally begged to have those golden brown eyes lock on her, but the beauty only had eyes for her posse. They continued past without acknowledging the prop crew. Jodi studied her departure as carefully as she had her approach, needing that tight ass in the palm of her hands. Oh, what she could do with that lethal swing.

Amelia pinched her arm.

Jodi snapped out of her heated trance and covered the stinging spot with her hand. "Ouch, you violent woman! What was that for?"

"I suggest you pull that tongue back in your mouth before I snap it out with my pliers." Amelia jabbed her finger toward the makeshift work area where her progress was already evident. Jodi spotted a two-foot-high wooden pedestal and lots of long, thin sticks. "Get your billboard ass over there. Now!"

Jodi pursed her lips but started walking, rubbing the soon to be bruise on her forearm. "Jealous?"

"Move your ass, Connelly."

"Ooh, I love it when you call me that. Makes me all warm and fuzzy inside."

"The boric acid in my tool box will give the same effect. Move."

"With added sex stimulants? You're making me wet." Jodi glanced over her shoulder to make sure Amelia wasn't too close on her heels. She had a hell of a slap. "I might touch myself."

"The only thing you're going to be touching is props."

"Did you say a riding crop?" Jodi swerved around the props and a large toolbox, then turned to face her. "I never knew you had it in you, Amelia."

"Shut up and get to work."

"Aye, aye, boss lady." Jodi saluted her. "But I'll be thinking about you wielding that riding crop all day." She wiggled her brow as Amelia rolled her eyes and ducked to pick up an array of stiff plastic poles.

Jodi smiled. Life was great. Here she was with no fear of ever going hungry again, the most important person still in her life and making an honest woman out of herself. Amelia didn't miss too many chances to chastise Jodi about her chosen way of life or the array of women she kept on her schedule, the women Amelia claimed owned Jodi. That didn't make her care less, only more. Jodi disagreed with her assertion. The women she "dated" might stuff her bank account with large denominations, but they didn't own her. If anything, Jodi owned them. It was Jodi who supplied the sexual junkies their burning desires, kept them addicted to their fantasies. She was their drug.

Amelia's biggest argument was that the love of Jodi's life could have possibly already passed her by while she knelt between uncaring thighs. Was she right?

Jodi looked in the direction the bossy goddess had taken, and her crotch burned. Amelia would have a fit if she knew the erotic scenario running through her mind.

❖

Eve slid into a chair behind the card table for the second time that morning. "Silence, everyone!" she barked over the rushed voices of her coworkers. Everyone hushed at once. Angelica, Roger, and three of her assistants sat with her, their wary eyes searching to see if her five-minute break had cooled down her temper. Khandi stood at the end watching the models carefully, almost feverishly.

Hell week had begun, starting with a five a.m. conference call in her hotel suite with Drinadine, the talent agency out of Paris. Eve had already chosen twenty models she would pick over during the pre-walk in three weeks for Paris fashion week. Frank, the CEO and founder, insisted she make a solid decision on fifteen before she arrived. He made some excuse about other commitments for some of the models. Eve didn't give a shit. Either they wanted to wait it out to be part of one of the biggest fashion events of the year, or she would move on to some lesser venue. The choice was completely in their hands, and he had only wasted her morning shower time with nonsense, which only further pissed her off. She didn't like having her precious time interrupted, especially by a prick with ideas above his station. He hadn't liked being told that, either.

Running an hour behind schedule due to his pompous ass, she'd arrived at the studio only to have the normal raft of questions drilled at her. It had taken another hour to get everyone situated, which had kept her from introducing herself to Amelia, the owner of Ruccar, the new prop designer she'd hired on short notice for a trial run. Eve had been impressed with her credentials as well as the conference call. The woman had sounded strong and confident, a quality that was a must in her world. Now she'd have to see if the quality of her work outshined the competition.

And to top off her chaotic morning, a model had broken down in tears over a missing shoe. Eve had tried to have patience with her, allowing her extra time in her search while she went over the schedule with Roger and Khandi for the tenth time in two hours.

However, the more the model had cried, which only slowed her progress in the hunt, the more Eve's aggravation had increased. She'd had no choice but to snap and yell at the lot of them.

She slapped her hands on the table and rose. "This is a respectable fashion show, ladies, not a fucking prom. I don't have time for tears or dramatized hysterics. You who can't seem to keep up with my merchandise, leave." Eve ignored the model's loud sobs as she raced from the room and turned a glare on the remaining wide-eyed beauties. "The rest of you, take five minutes to get your shit together. When I get back, I want to see professionals standing before me. We have a show to put on in less than four days. Have I made myself clear?"

Angelica had scrambled for her BlackBerry, no doubt to replace the missing spot on the runway while Eve stormed from the room in search of a nutrition bar and to get her temper back in check. Dammit, not being able to call Lexi was making her a total bitch.

Now, as she looked over the models standing along the back wall like they were victims awaiting a firing squad, Eve felt calm and collected. "Okay, ladies, let's get this show on the road."

One by one, the models walked and posed. Eve matched their photos to the sketches she'd paired them with earlier. Out of the twelve, she only switched two. She passed each confirmed match to Angelica, who made notes before sharing the photos with the hair and makeup artists. The artists would create their own vision of makeup, hair, and jewelry they wanted to complete the ensemble.

Finally, the last model turned and exited the room. Eve sighed and leaned back in her chair, anxious and excited, yet trimmed with dread. Anything could happen at this point. The release of a model was proof of that. She usually coped with each malfunction, managing to maintain a degree of composure in the process, but for some reason, today, everything had gotten under her skin until she wanted to scream or break something.

She needed Lexi to take her in hand and soothe her frustration.

No. She didn't. What she needed was coffee, maybe another

breakfast bar, and to make sure progress was well under way with the other crews.

Eve pushed away from the table, reaching for the BlackBerry chirping by her side. She read the text from Gloria, the set director, stating they were ready for Eve to pick out her desired lighting for her spot in the show.

She replied that she'd be there shortly, then clipped the phone back to her side.

Angelica hung up and stood. "I have another model on the way. I'm sorry about—"

"No apologies necessary." Angelica nodded and Eve continued. "I have a concern about model number three. A bit on the skinny side. I'll use her, but I'd like to talk to her first, to explain how important her health is. Can you bring her to me in about thirty?"

"Absolutely."

"I'm going to make some rounds. We'll all connect over lunch, say, around twelve, to double-check progress. Text me when your new model is ready." Eve motioned for Khandi.

"She'll be here in about an hour."

"Excellent." Eve left the room and made her way toward Francesca, with Roger hot on her heels as if she might get away. Khandi matched her strides beside her.

"I need to check in on Francesca, then meet Gloria." Eve checked the time on her watch and quickened her steps. That son of a bitch had really messed up her morning, and Roger hadn't stopped scowling about it.

Khandi looked over her shoulder and puckered her lips. "I'll be over there joining the line of ladies drooling over your new prop designer when you need me."

Eve looked in the direction of the cubicles set up for the crews. "Is that very businesslike?"

"Who cares? She's flippin' hot." Khandi turned and strolled away.

Eve rolled her eyes and headed toward the wardrobe area with Roge right behind her. They turned down an adjoining hallway toward the area designated for Francesca, the models, and the overflow for wardrobe. Doors dotted the hall where models and makeup artists would soon fill the rooms. Today, the crowd was at a minimum since most crews were hard at work setting up individual show times. Soon, everything would change. The halls would be packed, every spare inch of space needed for last-second practice walks, with the hair and makeup artists scurrying after their appointed models so they didn't knock a single pin or hairpiece out of place.

Soon, the quiet halls would resemble a zoo. A beautiful, chaotic zoo. Eve thanked her lucky stars she was able to snag the perfect studio in the theater district. Everything she needed was within walking distance.

Leading the way into the crowded room, Eve found Francesca standing before one of the models, who was wrapped in the black and crimson gown. Francesca looked in her element with a pincushion clamped around one wrist and several pins wedged between her lips.

"I see you're already hard at work." Eve walked up behind her to get a closer look at the star creation. "Seeing it still takes my breath away."

Francesca used up the last of the pins in her mouth on the model's hips, then gave Eve a hug.

"Yes. It's beautiful." Francesca waved the model off the pedestal and her assistant took over helping her shed the glimmering gown.

Eve immediately thought of Zara, how stunning the dress would look on her lean curves. Zara bought every piece Eve created. Be it samples, or the hit of the runway, Zara would own them all. All Eve had to do was name the price.

That fact sometimes scared Eve. She wasn't dependent on Zara, or her money, but it sure didn't hurt her sales.

"I don't know what I'd do without you."

"You'd do the same thing you were doing without me. Starving." Francesca laughed, a deep baritone sound that was addicting.

Eve joined the laughter, gave Francesca another hug, then ducked out.

It seemed there was a hottie in the house. Eve was positive she'd need to be rescued from Khandi by now.

Chapter Six

E ve found Gloria at the end of the makeshift runway, her expression intent as she studied the lighting, exacting angles, and brightness. Her assistant pressed another button on the remote control and the lighting changed again. The aisle lit up with soft pale light.

"Eve, I'm not happy with this," Gloria said. "It's not bright enough."

Eve stood beside her. "I agree. Go back with the hard filter."

The light changed again; this time harsh white light landed on the catwalk. "Yes. That one."

Gloria nodded and gave a thumbs up to the assistant in the window above the stage.

Eve turned to leave and spotted one of the new props at the end of the newly erected makeshift runway. She went closer for an inspection and was pleased with the engraving spiraling from bottom to top of the knee-high pedestal. She could already envision the end product, chrome-speckled vases filled with curly twigs in metallic colors. In years past, she'd tried to use duller colors so that the gowns would stand out above all else. This year, she wanted something different to showcase the sparkle she'd added to over half of the designs.

It was then she realized she hadn't taken the time to introduce herself to the new prop designer, or rescue her, and she went in search of her. She found the designated area and spotted Khandi along with three other workers giggling like schoolgirls. "What are you guys up to?"

All but Khandi jumped and spun around. They stared at Eve as if she might bite, then scurried away.

"Khandi. What the hell are you doing?"

Without turning around, Khandi shushed her. "I told you. Ogling the new hottie."

"Can you pretend to act your age?" Eve waved for Roger. "Let's go meet this new prop goddess."

Khandi gave a tiny squeal, then dodged around Eve and led the way into the enclosed area.

Eve shook her head and followed Khandi into a small area sectioned off at the side of the temporary catwalk and found two women laughing and jostling each other like kids at summer camp. It was cute, actually. Only problem was, they were on her clock, and time was of the essence during hell week.

"Amelia?" Eve grinned as the woman whipped around as if she'd heard a gunshot, while the other woman turned with such casual ease that Eve wondered if she were high on paint fumes.

Khandi sucked in a startled breath and Eve could understand why. The taller woman was a breathtaking creature for sure. Eve's insides heated.

Dressed as if she'd recently stepped right off a highway billboard, the woman's appearance screamed suave control. And fuck me. Her white button-down shirt was still perfectly pressed and bright, the rolled-up sleeves giving Eve a clear view of tight forearms. Eve couldn't help noticing clean nails and strong hands. Dark jeans encased well-muscled legs and hugged her thighs like a second skin. Her short, straight brown hair was damn enticing the way it fell in disarray like there was no rhyme or reason to the style. Eve was sure it'd look even better between her thighs, sifting through her fingers while she yanked the woman tight against her pussy.

Ivy green eyes turned her way and Eve had to remind herself that she wasn't a fish, that she needed air to survive.

She calmly refilled her lungs, wondering if they bred women this sexy in London, and if so, how she'd been in all the wrong places every year she'd been putting on the event. What fun she could have been having with this hunk of rare meat a few hundred times a week, twice a year.

From her tan loafers all the way up to that unkempt hair, the woman was all butch. Just like her fantasy woman, the one she kept buried deep in the recesses of her mind. She had been positive no such specimen existed, until now. Too bad she lived across the world. Too bad Eve would only have a week to get to know her, to feel those fingers plunge deep.

"I'm Amelia, owner of Ruccar," the other woman blurted, breaking the trance. She tugged off a thick rubber glove and extended her hand to Eve.

"It's great to meet you, Amelia. I'm Eve Harris." Eve pulled her attention away from the sexy barbarian and shook her hand, pleased with the confident grip. If there was one thing that irked her, it was women who felt inferior in this line of work. This was a fuck and be fucked world, and usually only the strong fought their way to the surface. Eve would know. She'd hand-battled a lot of competition and thankfully come out the victor.

Ms. Tall and Handsome made a sharp noise much like Khandi's and Eve cut a glance back on her. The woman quickly turned away, but the gesture didn't go unnoticed by Amelia, who quirked a warning brow before smiling again.

"This is Jodi. I conned her into working with me this week."

Jodi. Eve liked that name. It fit the tempting butch. Eve wondered how well those muscular thighs would fit between her spread thighs, how smooth that tongue would curl around her aching clit.

Eve nodded in her direction but didn't offer her hand and neither did Jodi. She wondered what the exchange was all about but was truly out of time for small talk. Angelica should be calling soon, and Roger was already breathing heavy with impatience. "Nice to meet you."

Khandi's BlackBerry chirped, mocking Eve.

"I'm sorry I didn't get a chance to introduce myself earlier. The prop is beautiful. Did you—"

"Eve, the model you wanted to talk to is on her way," Khandi announced.

Eve turned to look at her, pouring out her aggravation in a single look. "Thank you, *Khandi*."

Khandi shrugged and tapped the phone. "I'm just saying."

Eve looked back at Amelia, resisting another glance at the

assistant, who she could see out of the corner of her eye was looking everywhere but in her direction. "Did you get the memo about the new color scheme?"

Roger's phone chirped. "Eve, one of the models is refusing to wear—"

Eve held up her hand to silence him. "Do not use the word *refuse* in front of me today. Send her ass home and have Angelica replace her." She sighed and gave Amelia an apologetic shrug.

"Yes, I did. The prop's not complete. I had Jodi take it out to make sure the height was correct." Amelia nodded toward her. "I decided not to paint until I was sure no more changes would be made."

"That's probably wise." Eve wanted to add that at least someone around there was thinking ahead. She liked Amelia already. As well as her yummy assistant.

"Eve, Angelica said—"

Once again, Eve held up her hand. She was used to being interrupted and having to fix five hundred problems while managing to hold up an intelligent conversation, but right now, she wanted total silence to soak up the moment, to inhale the musky scent that could only belong to the delicious assistant Jodi.

"When do you expect to have the other three props ready?"

"I'll have a second finished in about three hours. The remaining two will be ready tomorrow afternoon. That gives me the following day to paint and make any final adjustments you want."

"Perfect." Eve noticed the model standing uneasily a few feet away. She nodded her acknowledgment in her direction. "Amelia, Jodi, it's been a pleasure. I'll check back in later today to see the progress." She took one last glance at Jodi then walked away.

Jodi stared at Eve's retreating back, at the delicate shape of her ribs, at the dangerous curves of her hips and ass and thighs, shocked to the core, her body heat spiking.

That voice. Eve's voice. Her Eve, right here in London.

She hadn't needed to hear Eve's name roll off that tongue to know who she was. She'd know that voice anywhere. She'd heard it a hundred times over the wire with her eyes closed, fighting for control, hundreds more in her dreams, where she could lose that grip. Whispering, whimpering, and crying out her name, she'd heard every aspect of the delicate sound.

Worse, the impulse to fuck her had been consuming, drowning her as Eve made small talk with Amelia. She was perfect all the way down to those worn-out boots.

She'd never been so confused in her life, not even when the police had showed up on her doorstep to announce that her mother wouldn't be coming home. Ever. While the men had stood tall in the living room of the rented apartment, waiting for her to pack a bag, waiting to haul her to social services. Warning bells had screeched loud. With her bag looped over her back, she'd climbed out the bathroom window and run like hell.

Even with memories slashing through her mind, Jodi could feel Amelia's penetrating stare and avoided looking at her. Instead, she focused on Eve's raven curls nestled against the middle of her back as Eve stood less than ten feet away with the too thin model Jodi had followed into the theater that morning.

Everything rushed at her at once—Eve always working, always rushing, always tired, and always lonely. She was positive now that Eve didn't have time to make friends, let alone relationships. The picture was crystal clear.

Eve was large and always in charge. She was queen of her fashion world. It turned Jodi on—all that control and power on the outside, losing it freely on the inside with Lexi's voice coaxing her to a screaming orgasm. Jodi knew Eve, knew what she sounded like when she was coming and powerless. She knew how sweet her name sounded pouring over those lips.

"Care to share what the hell that was all about?"

"Shhh." Jodi strained to hear Eve's conversation.

"I told Angelica I'd use you in the show, but I advise you not to fall into the trap of watching body fat and calories. Your health should be the most important thing to you, not your fame."

Jodi swallowed as the two women started walking again. They slowly disappeared, absorbed in the sea of staff. People raced toward Eve, stopping her every few feet.

Amelia stepped in front of Jodi, blocking her locked view on Eve. Had she just heard that right? A fashion designer telling a model that she was too skinny. What were the odds? It made Jodi want to fuck her all the more.

"Hello! I'm talking to you."

"It's her." Jodi forked her fingers through her hair, her mind muddled, her body aching.

"Who?"

"Eve."

"Yeah? Eve…my new boss. What about her?" Amelia waved her hands in front of Jodi's face. "Earth to Jodi."

Jodi blinked, finally snapping back to reality, and whispered, "She's one of my phone clients."

Amelia threw her head back and laughed so hard people stopped their work to investigate. "In your fucking dreams, Ms. Walking Advertisement." She gave a final snort, shaking her head, and then lowered her voice. "Did you happen to see her? *All* of her? From head to toe, that woman reeks of sex. Why in the world would she need you, a sex operator? Especially a pretend Brit halfway across the map? Again, did you *see* her?"

"It's her, Amelia."

"If you say that one more time I'm going to take my chisel and work a masterpiece on your brassy balls. I'm so not kidding." Amelia smirked and turned to look back at Eve. "You're full of shit, Jodi. No way would someone that sexy have a need for a damn sex phone operator."

Jodi's pussy throbbed. The moment felt surreal. After all those nights wondering what Eve would look like, if she were grotesque or hideous, and now she was looking at this breathtaking creature. She was reality at its finest. All the phone calls, with her eyes screwed tight, resisting the desperate urge to touch herself and follow Eve into the erotic abyss.

Amelia turned sharply. "Completely coincidental. Just your wishful thinking. Come on. Let's get back to work." She ducked around Jodi and squatted next to the newest prop they'd been working on.

Her insides clenched. She wanted to be Eve's living fantasy, wanted to do all those things she promised over a phone, all the things she made Eve envision as she fucked herself.

Jodi knelt next to Amelia. "It's her."

"It's not her."

The challenge was in her voice, that finality of the conversation. "I can prove it."

Amelia sat down Indian-style and faced Jodi. "How so?"

"She has a tattoo of a dragon on her left shoulder blade. Or so she said."

"Well, Sherlock, getting women to shed their clothes is your specialty, not mine. Stop this nonsense. You're full of shit. Quit fantasizing and use those biceps to move that prop over to the runway."

What a delicious scenario that was—getting Eve to drop her pants, to hear how sweet those mewls of passion would sound against her mouth and tongue. She wanted, yearned, and ached to fuck her.

She needed to press their naked bodies together just one time.

Without a doubt, Jodi knew she was going to fuck the fashion mogul, the woman who sought her voice several times a week, before this so-called hell week ended.

On that, she'd bet her entire fortune.

CHAPTER SEVEN

E ve pulled the navy blue thigh-high dress over her head, then wiggled it down over her hips and pushed up her breasts.

"There you go. Push the girls out. Zara will love them staring back at her all night." Khandi mocked her from her sitting position in the middle of Eve's bed.

Eve gasped and released her hold, then adjusted the deep scoop neck to minimize her cleavage. The last thing she wanted was Zara ogling her tits. Hell, come to think of it, the last thing she wanted was to be on a dinner date with her one-week fuck. Period.

Zara still brought in a trail of followers, all loaded with thick wads of cash. As promised, she would make nice with Zara for the sake of the sales. Even if that meant enduring an entire evening in her company for the resulting sales spike. She'd suffered worse opponents, though none that she'd fucked.

Satisfied, she'd tucked the "girls" securely back into place, Eve nodded approval and turned to face Khandi. "Will this do?" Eve held her arms to the side as she turned in a circle.

"Do for whom? Zara? She wants you out of your clothes, so she doesn't care what you wear or how you look in it." Khandi rolled onto her back and peeled the paper from a fruit roll-up. "By the way, did you notice the hottie with your new prop designer today?" She wiggled her brow suggestively. "Also, did you read the tabloid I left on your bathroom counter?"

"I don't read that shit. You know that." Eve stepped into a pair of cream pumps, fastened the inch-wide buckle around her ankle, and chose not to comment on the hottie in question.

Hot didn't begin to describe it.

"Well, you should. Might find something interesting happening around here." Khandi drew the length of the roll-up as far as her arm would allow, then started tugging the candy into her mouth with her tongue.

"I'm sure you'll bend heaven and hell to notify me of some earth-shattering news."

"Don't count on it. I saw the way your mouth watered over that fresh piece of meat today. If you could have, you would have fucked her where she stood," Khandi managed to mumble around the wad of goo. "Some things are better left untold. Especially if it gets my boss laid."

Eve picked up her matching clutch and checked her image in the mirror. "What does any of this have to do with…what were we talking about, a magazine? Or was it the hottie?"

"Both, actually." Khandi rolled onto her stomach, her ankles locking in the air behind her.

"You're confusing me. And for the love of kittens, stop eating that crap. I bet your dentist loves you for paying half his mortgage." Eve snatched up the hotel keycard and started for the door. "And stop watching porn on my TV. The thought of you masturbating in my bed grosses me out."

"Why? That's what you'll be doing later when your might-be-sexy, might-not-be, Lexi purrs you into an orgasm. Oh, God, Lexxxxiiiiii!" Khandi sang, then broke into hysterical laughter as Eve let herself out of the suite and slammed the door.

She stomped toward the elevator, questioning her morals for sharing facts about Lexi with that gum-chewing, roll-up-addicted witch of an assistant.

Eve pressed the Down button and waited, wondering what Lexi was doing right now. Somewhere in this very city, she lived and breathed. She could be having dinner with her parents, or tearing up a dance floor with a date. She could be fucking someone.

The thought chilled her and she tapped her foot impatiently. How could she be jealous of a voice? Sure, the voice was connected to a real person, but not anyone Eve would ever meet in person. What was wrong with her? She was seriously addicted to a fucking sex operator.

It was disturbing, yet just as Khandi said—it would be to Lexi's voice she would crawl after this dreaded dinner with Zara was over.

And speaking of the hottie, Jodi, what had been up with her? She'd acted weird, almost as if she recognized Eve. That wasn't a hard assumption, seeing as her face was pretty well known in the fashion world. However, the woman didn't strike her as fashion-obsessed. Well, minus the suave way her clothing had adorned that tight body. Besides the natural way she dressed herself and misbehaved with her boss, she looked completely out of her element.

Eve wanted to misbehave with her, wanted to open herself wide, wanted to touch herself while Jodi watched, wanted to soak in the sight of Jodi soaking in the sight of her fucking herself. She wanted Jodi to fall on her naked flesh, wanted Jodi's weight crushing her, dominating her, taking and claiming her in every way a woman could.

The elevator door opened and Eve rushed inside, anxious to get Zara out of her hair for the night so she could get back to her suite, back to her bed, back to her phone. To Lexi.

She licked her lips as that voice cluttered her thoughts. Lexi would be able to take away the growly aftereffects that would surely be present after this damn meet-and-greet with Zara was complete. A shudder ran through her as she recalled their night together, naked, sweaty, Eve unsure and way out of her element in the hands of a femme. Her flight home had been quiet, to Khandi's dislike, pondering her sanity, and missing rough, butch hands.

It had taken her barely twenty-four hours after arriving home to find a willing partner—a willing butch—and she'd fucked her like it was her last three hours alive. God, it'd been so long since she'd felt the power of a tight female between her thighs, bucking into her, her body a bundle of muscles as Eve thrashed against her. She'd needed strong hands, athletic backs, and powerful legs to level her off her feet, to make her forget the soft hands that had traveled over her body.

Her pussy heated as she recalled the butch fucking her standing up, the dildo stabbing into her, how she'd made Eve claw at the air and scream for God.

It was that kind of powerful embrace and orgasms that she could only get from a butch. They were so cocky and sure of themselves, usually with good reason.

Eve shook her head.

Now on the main floor, Eve headed into the dining room and spotted Zara immediately. She stood out from the crowd of socialites with her hair piled high on her head in an array of old-fashioned waves dotted with diamond-studded pins. Lipstick transformed her plump lips into dark red cherries, her high cheekbones hinted with rouge and her eyes emphasized by thick black lashes.

Eve stood for a long minute, wondering exactly what she could have ever been so curious about. Jesus, she was so femme. The opposite of the type of woman Eve fantasized about in her waking dreams.

Eve needed butch, butch, and all fucking butch.

Zara looked up and spotted her. A genuine smile formed on her mouth, but there were no flirty winks, not even a spark of desire in her eyes. Eve expelled a long breath in relief. Whatever had arced between them was gone. Thank the fashion Gods.

Eve went to her and placed a token kiss on her cheek. She knew that was expected.

"You look absolutely stunning, Eve. That new tan looks delicious on you," Zara purred.

Eve liked the tan as well. Khandi had fought her tooth and nail about spray tans until Eve had thrown up her hands and decided to go for it. Now it was routine, as were the massages she worked in on her lunch break. It wasn't as relaxing as she felt after Lexi's voice had coaxed her to climax, but it was damn sure close.

"Thank you. How have you been?" Eve scoured the room, nodding and smiling as she recognized faces. Then she came to a face that hit something solid in her chest and she had to sit.

Jodi. She sat three tables down and across. Opposite her was an older woman who wasn't ashamed of her love for diamonds. At least three rings laden with bling sparkled on the hand wrapped around her wine glass.

How cute. She was taking her mother out to dinner. Eve thought of her own mother, who'd called less than two hours ago to update her on their whereabouts. After her dad retired, her parents had opted to sell the house in which she'd grown up and buy an RV. They'd been traveling ever since. It was so their style, to just up and sell off their belongings, then hit the road with nothing more than an atlas and a

GPS. This week they were hunkering down in Amarillo, Texas, where they had visited the Cadillac Graveyard along the famous Route 66.

So precious and so not Eve. Her mother had chosen the role of loving stay-at-home slave. She'd given up any dreams of a career to be at her husband's beck and call, to carpool, to hustle a cheerleading squad to and from practices and games. Eve couldn't. Eve wouldn't. It might do for her mother, but she'd be damned if she'd give up herself for another. She'd worked too damn hard to toss it to the wind.

"I've been fantastic. Traveling. Seeing and being seen. I'm sure you can imagine."

Eve wanted to turn her attention back to Zara, but she couldn't pull her raging hormones away from Jodi's hard profile and that damn hair that once again looked like she'd rushed a towel through it after a shower. It definitely shouldn't be that sexy. Well, not off a cover, anyway. But it was, and Eve wanted her thighs clamped around the strands, wanted her legs dangling over those broad shoulders, wanted to come in her mouth.

She struggled for control and finally turned back to Zara. "Sounds like you've been busy."

Zara faked modesty with a slight wave of her hand, then quickly recovered and angled her face toward the ceiling. "It is good to be me sometimes."

Eve mentally cursed. Not only was Zara all femme, but she was all femme wrapped inside herself. She was sure if Zara could date and fuck herself without having to use her own energy, she'd have found the perfect soul mate.

"I hear through the grapevine you have a priceless new design. I can't wait to get my hands on it. It will be stunning on me, I'm positive." Zara's eyes twinkled.

Could anyone be more stuck on themselves if they tried?

Eve looked back to Jodi, trying to size up the weird interaction earlier in the day. The second greeting hadn't gone any better, this time with Jodi strolling away while Eve and Amelia went over the paint colors. It had been unsettling to watch her deliberately stay away from her. She was clearly not interested. The action only fueled Eve's desire to fuck her, to show her how dangerous being inside her could be. God, she wanted to tear her apart with her teeth.

Without taking her eyes off the sexy piece of ass, Eve answered. "Yes, you're going to look absolutely stunning in it."

Jodi turned and trapped Eve in a carnal stare, her pretty eyes dipping from Eve's cleavage to her legs, her expression hungry and searching. Eve swallowed hard, every fiber of her body awakening. Then Jodi looked away, her full attention back on the woman. Eve waited, hoping to get another chance to feel those eyes penetrate her soul, but it seemed that brief glance was all she was going to be privy to.

Not even a smile? Or a wink? What? Was she dog meat and Khandi forgot to tell her? Khandi didn't hesitate to point out a flaw in anyone, Eve especially. That complete dismissal bugged her, though she was positive it shouldn't. It never had before.

She didn't think of herself as egotistical, but she'd turned a head or two in her time. Yet she couldn't hold this woman's attention for even six fucking seconds. Eve was suddenly jealous of the woman sitting across from Jodi. Whoever she was, she practically owned Jodi's focus. Eve wanted to be the one locked in that ivy stare, wanted to dominate her attention.

Thirty minutes later, Eve had found the strength not to keep looking Jodi's way by enduring Zara's dramatized conversation about nightclubs and overzealous catfights.

Eve finished her salad and pushed it away. "I think that was the biggest concoction of tossed greens I've ever seen. Not to mention delicious."

Zara watched her curiously. "I don't think I've ever witnessed anyone devouring a salad that big before. Everything okay? You seem a little distracted."

Eve thought the statement odd. Zara didn't strike her as one to offer a morsel of pity. "Sorry. I am a little. Seems I don't have a minute to breathe this week."

"The work mule is admitting she's tired?" Zara looked around with a worried look. "Will the ceiling fall in on us?" She giggled and patted Eve's hand.

Eve shrugged. "You caught me. Maybe I'm getting old?"

Zara gasped and delicately covered her heart. "You know that word is a no-no, Eve Harris. We don't get o—that word." She puckered her lips and readjusted herself in the seat.

Eve laughed and nodded. "You will never age, sweetie."

Motion drew Eve's attention to Jodi's table. Jodi subtly called for the waiter with a wave of her finger to have her date's wine refilled. God, how she looked at her date. It was like…like a lover.

No way. No way in hell something as fine as that would be fucking an old hag. Absofuckinglutely no way.

Once again, a jealous knot formed. Sex. That was it. She was lacking sex, phone sex, and Lexi was only a call away. She could and would put Eve out of her misery. Just a little more time with Zara, listening to her go on and on about herself, and she could escape the madness, could climb into bed with that British accent cradled to her ear.

She took a hard look at Zara, taking in the edges of her small breasts visible in the deep vee of her blouse, then blinked hard in surprise. What the fuck was she thinking? Shit, if she seriously thought Zara could scratch this itch, she was warped.

She jerked her concentration away just in time to see Jodi and her date rise from the table. The casual way Jodi placed her hand at the small of the woman's back had Eve swallowing a gasp. The woman wrapped her hand around Jodi's elbow like a perfect Scarlett O'Hara against her beau.

And if their touches weren't proof enough, their path to the elevator was enough to make Eve throw up a little in her mouth.

Sweet angels, was she seriously going to take that wrinkle-faced woman upstairs and fuck her? The thought was unnerving. It was downright disgusting. More than disgusting. Eve's pussy spasmed.

Eve was mesmerized with their departure, though her stomach was coiling like a rattler. She was aware of Zara's voice, of Jodi's sure strut across the room, of heat cradling between her thighs. Jodi allowed the woman into the elevator first, then stepped in behind her. She pushed a button, then turned and trapped Eve in a clit-massaging stare.

Eve swallowed hard and whipped around to face Zara, her heart jackhammering against her chest.

A grin crept across Zara's lips and then she purred, "My, my. What expensive taste you have, my dear."

Eve forced herself to stop this foolish behavior. She was acting irrational and jealous. She couldn't think of being jealous a day in her life, let alone irrational. Her career, the well-being of her career, depended highly on her rationality.

Fuck! She needed Lexi. Needed Lexi to whisk her into a back-arching orgasm.

"What's that supposed to mean?"

Zara glanced over Eve's shoulder, then looked at her throat. "Your necklace. It looks expensive."

Eve self-consciously fingered the glass pendant hanging in the hollow of her throat. "It's not."

As quickly as possible, Eve made her excuses and then staggered into an elevator. For some reason, she felt scarred after witnessing something so sexy taking that old bat upstairs. The thought of that woman pumping beneath Jodi made her inner demon growl and scratch at the surface.

Eve ripped open her clutch and dug out her cell.

She just needed Lexi. That's all.

Lexi would fix her, would soothe this burning itch.

She always did.

CHAPTER EIGHT

Jodi's heart cramped as the elevator doors hissed to a close, cutting off the sight of Eve. Of the shock and confusion clouding her gorgeous amber eyes. Had that been acknowledgment or disappointment nestled in their depths? Hell, Eve was dining with Zara. If her cover wasn't already blown, she was positive it would be very soon, probably within minutes. The bitch had been a client on too many occasions, and the grapevine started and ended on her too-red lips.

Shit! Now what? All those images of fucking Eve, all the desires to hear those satisfied cries against her flesh, would flutter apart and evaporate before she hit the tenth floor. Eve would know she was an escort.

The thought drove a nail through her. Suddenly, she didn't want to go upstairs, didn't want to be a paid whore tonight. The thought of undressing this woman, Marilyn, put a sour taste in her mouth, in her heart, in her soul. She didn't want to lay her hands on Marilyn's body. Not tonight. Not when Eve's eyes were haunting her.

When the door opened, it was all Jodi could do to step out, to lead the way to a room, to a bed, where someone else would come by her hands. An uneasy nausea settled in the pit of her stomach.

She walked to the hotel room on heavy feet and locked the door behind them. This was her life. The life she'd chosen for herself. This was the consequence of her choices so many years ago.

Marilyn let her pashmina wrap fall to the floor as she walked toward the bed. Jodi shucked out of her jacket and turned her back on the view of Marilyn preparing for sex. She concentrated on Eve, those striking amber eyes, her curves, her mouth, her voice. What would she sound like in person when Jodi stroked an orgasm from the pits of her soul? How would she feel pulsing around Jodi's tongue? Jodi wanted to undress her, fold her hands around plump breasts, and explore every inch of her body before slipping inside her quivering depths.

She closed her eyes as she dropped the jacket over the chaise lounge, her body spiking with heat and the imaginary feel of Eve's flesh in her hands. Her heart sagged that no such quest would be possible once the truth emerged. By now, Zara would surely have blurted out the facts, no doubt embellished with her own brand of malicious poison, and tomorrow, Eve wouldn't look at Jodi the same. Those curious eyes hadn't gotten past Jodi earlier today. She was interested. Or had been.

When Marilyn cooed behind her, Jodi stiffened and drew in an unsteady breath.

With her head held high, she turned around and found Marilyn perched on the end of the bed. With her mind twisted, she started toward her. It wasn't the first time she'd been Marilyn's boi toy. God save her, she knew it wouldn't be the last.

She kept walking. She had to finish this, no matter what.

One step at a time, she forced herself to approach the bed.

Marilyn smiled and lay back, her favored position.

Jodi knew them all so well, each and every client, their fantasies, their desires, what made them cry, what made them scream, what made them rupture with relief.

Right now, she didn't care that Marilyn wanted a hot mouth latched on to her, or that Suzanne preferred Jodi to take her from behind, or even that Emily liked to be handcuffed, then fingered until she expelled an orgasm. She didn't much care about anything except getting the job done so she could get the hell out of this claustrophobic room and to the phone that would link her with a woman who had touched something deep inside, one call after another, one soft pant and lonely cry after another.

She reached the bed, knelt, pushed Marilyn's dress up around her thighs, and slowly removed her underwear with shaky hands. Gently, yet quickly, she placed kisses along the inside of her legs until she reached her wet opening. Normally, she'd tease until Marilyn begged to be taken. Not tonight. Not when Eve might still seek out Lexi's voice. If Zara hadn't demolished all hope, that is.

With her eyes screwed tight and her mind filling with the vision of Eve, she fastened her mouth around Marilyn's clit and sucked, much faster than Marilyn liked.

Marilyn didn't seem to notice her haste. She twisted and arched her back, then thankfully soon let out a low, dull cry, pumping against Jodi's face.

Jodi remained where she was, mechanically flicking Marilyn's clit with the tip of her tongue, until Marilyn stilled, and her legs hung limply around Jodi's shoulder.

This was her job. Her way of life. Her act of survival.

It was the only way she knew.

❖

Eve darted into the studio and stopped to shake the rain off the umbrella. She'd never felt droplets so cold. Bone chilling cold, yet so crisp and fresh, and if it were possible, she could smell it. The thought made her cringe. Since when did she give a shit if the rain had an odor, or if it was crisp? Never, that's when. It was fucking cold, and wet, and putting a damper on the beginning of her day.

A little aggravated to be cold and soaked all at the same time, she tossed the umbrella in the corner and shed the trench coat to find her shirt was wet as well. Sheesh. No wonder she was shaking like a leaf. Hugging her body, she stepped farther into the throng of workers to get her day started. Same shit, different day. She was unusually stressed for first thing in the morning, probably because Lexi hadn't answered her call. Hell, who was she kidding? It was definitely because Lexi hadn't answered. She'd needed her, wanted that alluring voice, yet all she'd gotten was that damn recorded message saying sorry she couldn't make it to the phone, please call back soon. This wasn't the first time she'd missed her, or rather, needed her. And since when did she need anyone? Never, was the answer. Yet she could feel the need bunched in her gut like a lump of lead. Where had it stemmed from? And why? And why did she fucking care right now? She was about to be drilled with a million questions as soon as someone realized she'd arrived. There wasn't time to ponder what the hell her hormones were up to lately. Lexi's personal and business life was of no concern to her.

Eve spotted Khandi with Roger across the room and headed their way. She needed coffee and warmth and the fucking rain to cease before she left this building again. Rain was one thing, but cold, damp, biting cold rain was quite another. Why hadn't she noticed in all the other years she'd been to London? Had work consumed her entire life so much that everything else around faded into the background? Including running across a woman as sexy as Jodi?

Khandi turned at her approach and checked her from head to toe. "Want me to find you a bar of soap?"

Eve quirked a brow at her. "Want me to find a new assistant?"

"My, my. Aren't we in a pissy mood? Phone signal zap out on you last night or something?"

"Zip it, lint licker."

Roger burst out laughing while Khandi rolled her eyes and walked away.

"How's the schedule looking for the day?" Eve attempted to peel the shirt away from her breasts and stomach for a few seconds, aware her nipples were tight and hard, then ran her fingers through her long hair to shake off the droplets.

"Final walk-through in an hour. Press interview at the church at two. Phone conference with Paris at three." He sighed. "Going to be a tight day."

"Always is." Eve scanned the room and found Amelia and Jodi squatted over a pedestal that gleamed with speckled chrome paint. Her nipples puckered into a more painful tip as Jodi stretched out for a tool, the muscles in her back drawing tight in her T-shirt.

Eve wasn't sure which she liked better—the walking advertisement in that sleek button-down she'd been sporting yesterday that had her mind ripping the shirt open, or a T-shirt she'd have to slide her hands up and inside. Either way, the woman was a gorgeous specimen to admire.

She barely drew her attention away when Khandi shoved a dry T-shirt at her. God bless her soul, she had coffee too.

Eve practically snatched the foam cup from her grasp to wrap her palms around the warmth for a long sip. "Thank you, thank you, thank you."

"I laced it with rat poison." Khandi smirked.

"I'd expect nothing less of you." Eve walked to the nearest table and set the cup down, then peeled the wet shirt over her head, not caring who saw her in a lace bra. She slipped into the dry one and attempted to fluff out her limp curls.

When she turned back around, she found Jodi and Amelia staring at her. Amelia looked like someone had punched her in the gut, her eyes wide and her mouth slightly open. Had her expression been anything but on the verge of horrified, Eve might have mistaken the wide-eyed look for lust. But she knew lust when she saw it, and right now, that particular expression rested on Jodi's face. She almost wore a satisfied smirk while her gaze dripped down Eve's frame.

Eve could think of a few other ways to give someone that kind of expression, and it usually started exactly like that—with her clothes coming off. She gave them a wave and the trance was broken. They both hustled back to work.

What the hell was up with those two?

Eve turned back to her coffee and found Khandi grinning like a fool. "What?"

"Nothing. Nothing at all."

"There's never nothing at all going on with you. Ever." Eve grabbed the cup and her wet shirt and headed into the throng of her day. "Let's get a move on."

❖

Many hours later, the day was finally coming to a close. The staff had dwindled to just Eve and Francesca and her assistant. Even Roger had left, which was unusual since he'd been Eve's shadow all day. Khandi had bolted about an hour ago, mumbling something about a café, and much-needed calories. Eve welcomed the quiet. It was a nice change to her hectic day.

Eve dropped into the chair while Francesca draped a gown on a hanger. "My whole body hurts."

"Are you getting excited? Show's in two days." Francesca stood back to examine the finished designs then nodded to her assistant.

"It's always exciting. Year after year." Eve wanted to add that this year seemed particularly exciting with a butch to steal glances at.

She recalled the flip-flop her stomach had done last night while the gorgeous hunk of burning lust disappeared into an elevator. There had to be some misunderstanding. There was no way a butch as fine as that would fuck that woman, a woman who had at least fifteen or more years on her. No way. Eve refused to believe anything other than the woman was an old acquaintance. Maybe Jodi was being the perfect gentleman, had wanted to escort the woman to her room unharmed. Yes, the perfect, sexy—*God I want to fuck her*—gentleman. That was the answer.

Her pussy spasmed and Lexi's voice hummed in the back of her mind. She needed relief after the rushed high. Lexi would put out the flame with that smooth accent.

"Let's all call it a day." Eve shoved out of the chair, needing the seclusion of her hotel room, needing Lexi's voice coaxing her into a hard orgasm.

"I still have some work to do. Go get some rest." Francesca pulled one of the dresses down and spread it across the table.

Guilt plagued Eve. Here she was ready to bolt for phone sex, and Francesca was still in work mode, all for Eve. The woman was a bigger workhorse than Eve was, if that were possible.

"Are you sure? I can hang around to help if you need." Eve prayed she didn't need her. She had a voice she desperately needed to get to.

"Positive. We've got this under control."

Oh, what a phone call she was going to make. Right after a hot bath. Damn, her feet hurt. "Okay, then I'm out of here."

"See you in the morning." Francesca waved her away.

With a final salute, Eve rushed back through the peaceful studio. She only stalled long enough to glance through the glass doors. It was raining. Again.

Lexi. Right now, she just needed Lexi. She scanned the corner where she'd left her umbrella to find it empty.

With a huff, she pushed through the double doors and stopped to examine the distance between the studio and the hotel and all the awnings along the way. It looked like she was going to get wet, whether she liked it or not. She could dive into a hot shower before she called Lexi, then get soaked with a different kind of wet.

The thought made her smile. A light breeze bristled across her cheeks. Something about the odor drew her out from under the awning and into the droplets. Was it even possible to smell rain? Lexi loved the rain.

She closed her eyes and inhaled the crisp, clean smell. Isn't that what Lexi had said? The rain made her feel alive. Made her feel clean. While the rain slicked across her cheeks, she could understand the meaning behind those words. There really was something cleansing about it, something uplifting and earthy.

With another deep breath, Eve opened her eyes and found Jodi on the sidewalk watching her and waiting.

Jodi had never seen anyone more breathtaking. The fact that Eve had just enjoyed a moment of the rain made her heart flutter. Her Eve hated the rain. Her Eve's life was too rushed to pause and inhale crisp, clean rain. Her Eve was standing in front of her, looking edible in that tight T-shirt that was darkening under the fat droplets of water, in tight jeans, and those fuck-me boots, in the drizzling rain, in the fucking flesh.

She stepped forward. "I was still in the neighborhood. Saw you come out and thought I'd walk you back to your hotel, if that's okay?" Jodi lied as she cringed to hear her natural Texas drawl. She'd been standing on the damn curb since Amelia had left the studio, warning her to go home, to avoid all thoughts of seducing her new boss, something Amelia knew she was without power to do. So she stayed and waited for any sign of Eve, praying she'd exit alone.

And here she was, those curious eyes eating Jodi alive. Jodi had to remind herself that she wasn't on the phone, that she didn't need to switch on the accent, and that Eve really wasn't a figment of her imagination.

With a quirk of that razor-sharp brow, Jodi was sure Eve would tell her to go fuck herself. She'd spent the first hour of her day on edge, worried that Eve would take one look at her and disgust would shadow her expression. And why wouldn't she? She'd basically witnessed Jodi escorting her date away for a fuck with Zara right there to prove any assumptions. What Jodi hated more than she dared admit was the fact that for once in her life, she'd wanted to be anyone else but herself, anything other than a paid whore.

But she hadn't gotten a look of disgust. Quite the opposite. Eve had looked at her with lust in her eyes, right after she'd pulled on the dry shirt, and right after she and Amelia had gotten a clear view of the vivid dragon cascading over her left shoulder blade. Dear God, it'd been pure, I want to fuck you, lust-filled eyes. Jodi wanted to fuck her so hard, wanted to be her living, breathing fantasy come to life. She wanted to lick that tattoo while she pushed inside her from behind.

"So you really do speak. Quite a shock to expect something British and hear, what, Arizona? Texas?"

"Texas, born and raised." Jodi took a few more steps toward her, still waiting for her answer.

When Eve stepped forward, staring up at Jodi with those same inquisitive eyes she'd worn last night during dinner, Jodi shook off her inner turmoil, held the umbrella over her head, and steered Eve in the direction of her favorite route along the Theatre District and Victoria Embankment.

Together, they walked quietly in the rain. She expected Eve to inquire where they were going, or why they'd taken the opposite route to her hotel, but no such question came Jodi's way. She liked that. The fact that Eve wasn't afraid of adventure. Just across the river, the London Eye revolved slowly. The lights reflected in the dark water below.

A corner vendor was closing down and Jodi persuaded him with a charming smile for two hotdogs. She was sure it had more to do with Eve's presence and the sexy wink she tossed his way. A memory came to mind of a too-thin teenager ordering a hot dog, then fishing in her scraggly jeans for change, knowing full well there wasn't a penny to find. Some would wave her away, hot dog intact. Others would bellow and threaten her with the law, as she ran like hell clutching her precious meal. How times had changed. And no matter how many hundreds she had in her wallet, she still loved these damn hot dogs.

"So tell me, what made you want to be a fashion designer?" Jodi had the impulse to whip her down on the sidewalk, in the nearest puddle, and fold herself in the warm alcove between her legs. She was losing her self-control in the closeness of Eve. What she wanted to know more was how Eve's voice had woven through her soul, how her sweet cries could rip her sanity in half.

"I've been designing clothes since my mother started my collection of Barbies. I'd cut their clothes to shreds, then sew them all back together with a plastic needle and yarn. Drove my mother insane.

But I had the coolest Barbies ever. I was the envy of my classmates." She gave a schoolgirl smile that made Jodi swallow.

She laughed to hide her nervousness, seeing that characteristic in Eve—always having to top everyone, driven to be the best. Jodi liked that feistiness, how Eve held her shit together when everything else around her seemed to be falling apart. She'd witnessed firsthand how Eve dominated her world. Better, she'd found a new appreciation for Eve when she carefully explained that the model needed to put meat on her bones.

They climbed the steps at the Houses of Parliament. Big Ben chimed the hour as they paused halfway across Westminster Bridge to look along the broad sweep of water toward Vauxhall.

"So if prop designing is just a hobby people have to con you into, what is your real job?" Eve tossed her napkin and paper in a nearby trash bin as they descended the steps to the riverside walk on the South Bank.

Jodi stiffened, needing Eve to believe she was something she wasn't. "I'd tell you, but then I'd have to kill you." She managed a chuckle.

"Hmm. Interesting. Like CIA stuff? FBI?" Eve stepped closer and Jodi had the impulse to wrap her arm around her shoulders as lovers would do. Wasn't that what they were, technically? Phone lovers.

"Can't say. Others could be listening."

Eve giggled and stepped close enough for their arms to press against each other.

Thankfully, they were almost in front of her apartment building close to the Albert Embankment. She concentrated on the erotic sound of Eve's heels clicking against the concrete while images of her naked, save for them draped over her shoulders, filled her mind. With a low grumble, she paused and turned to look up at her apartment. "This is me. Where I lay my head at night."

Eve looked up, her eyes wide with surprise as she took in the modern white steel and glass high-rise structure towering above them.

Jodi wondered why it was Lexi's voice Eve sought at night. Why was it Lexi she needed? Whatever the reason, Jodi felt lucky, proud, and miserably horny. She had whatever it was Eve wanted, obviously.

Eve looked so beautiful with her head upturned, her delicate throat exposed and vulnerable. Jodi wanted her. Needed her. Not just the voice on the other end of the line. She needed to be inside her, to feel those muscles clamp tight, to hear those moans caress her cheek, to wrench an orgasm from her body.

When Eve turned to look at her, Jodi had to swallow hard from the lust dancing in her eyes.

"Are you and Amelia a couple?"

"Oh no. Amelia's my best friend and straight as an arrow."

"Good. I don't do catfights."

Jodi couldn't stop staring at her, curious where the line of questions were heading. Eve's expression remained solid and unbridled.

"Now take me inside, then I want you to fuck me."

CHAPTER NINE

Jodi ushered Eve into the elevator with as much grace and confidence as she could muster. Fact was, she was scared shitless. She was more terrified right that second than she had been darting along the cold back alleys to outrun a rapist.

Could she be everything Eve wanted? Everything she needed? Lexi gave her those things, but could Jodi?

She'd never forget Eve admitting what her fantasy woman looked like, how excited and overwhelmed Jodi had been to have two of those factors. Green eyes and a rock-hard body—another factor that drove her to a sweat at the gym. The new hairstyle had come within weeks of Eve's confession, altering her slicked-back appearance to a carefree and unkempt style. She liked the new look, and so did the women, though she hadn't done it for her dates.

Come to think of it, why had she? For a woman she had never met? Would never set eyes on? To be the elusive fantasy, to know always that the woman Eve dreamed of existed? For some reason, it gave her a sick thrill to model herself on this imaginary person. To look in the mirror and see the woman Eve might crave.

Now in the flesh, what did it matter? Eve's fantasy woman was two steps away from her right that second, shaken to the core. Jodi prayed to a higher god that she could give Eve all she expected. Should she take charge like she did on the phone? Should she be gentle? Rough? This night had to be perfect, though she didn't know why. Eve would leave at the end of fashion week. Jodi would likely never see her face again.

They finally reached the fifteenth floor and she stepped out on shaky legs. She'd never been a nervous person, not even when sleep had eluded her for days and food was nowhere in sight. Right now, her nerves were flying apart.

With her gut churning, her pussy tight and ready, Jodi pushed the door open to her apartment, then stood back to allow Eve inside.

Eve looked cool as a cucumber, ready for whatever came her way. How did she do that? Act so calm and rational when something huge was about to unfold? Jodi wanted to rattle her composure, wanted to shake the very ground she stood on.

One look at that fine ass walking into the center of the foyer, with Eve scanning the surroundings, had Jodi out of her mind with need. She needed those cheeks in the palms of her hands, needed Eve's legs wrapped around her face, needed her tongue delving deep inside slick walls.

She shut the door and engaged the lock, then led Eve into the living quarters. "Care for something to drink?"

Eve went immediately to the windows, drawn, as everyone was, by the panoramic view of the Thames. "Later. After I work up a sweat."

That was an invitation if she'd ever heard one. Once again, Jodi swallowed hard. She opened her mouth to respond then realized there wasn't a verbal response.

She dropped the keys on the coffee table and stalked toward Eve, toward a woman who'd rattled her core with a soft whimper, who'd choked her composure with a helpless cry, and who now was about to do it all in person.

Eve turned slowly. Her body was nothing more than a silhouette against the expanse of glass, and her eyes were hot and smoldering as they bore at Jodi.

Imaginary hands shoved Jodi forward.

She closed the gap and walked Eve backward until she sealed her body against the glass. Eve's lips parted, expectant, her cinnamon breath ragged, needy.

Jodi lifted Eve's arms while feathering her fingers along the indentation of her elbow, forearm, stalling at her wrists. She opened her palms against Eve's and wove their fingers together, then pressed them against the glass as well.

She ducked and placed a kiss against her cheek, along her jawline, lifting her chin with the pressure.

Attuned to Eve's shallow breaths, Jodi lowered her mouth to her throat, inhaling a rich, floral scent, and slowly thrust against her. She sucked the flesh just beneath Eve's ear and ground harder, circling back, thrusting again.

Eve whimpered and lifted a leg around Jodi's hip, meeting her slow grind. "Is this a safe place to have sex?"

Jodi lifted her face from the warm alcove, acutely alerted by Eve's lips—pouty, full. She wanted to kiss her, wanted to slick her tongue inside that mouth and inhale the cries she'd only been privileged to hear over a phone before now. Respect held her in check. Self-respect. Eve was a client. Not in flesh form, but a client nonetheless.

"Safe for whom?" Jodi avoided her lips, more interested in all the sounds she could make fall from them. She kissed the space just beyond the corner of her mouth, held the spot for several seconds in agony to slip her tongue inside, before moving along the opposite jawline, dropping lower, licking, sucking, marking territory with a wet trail. She couldn't deny a kiss, but she couldn't instigate one either.

"Us...people watching." Eve swallowed and the movement rippled against Jodi's cheek. She angled her head back to open more flesh for Jodi.

Jodi took the opportunity and nipped. When Eve hissed, she licked away the sting. "The glass is mirrored. No one can see you...us." She bent her knees, then drove upward.

Eve tightened her grip against Jodi's hands and released a soft whine, lifting her other leg around Jodi's hip. She wiggled her fingers free and groped down Jodi's back, leaving Jodi's hands flat against the cold window. She pumped slowly against her and finally found refuge with a rough grip on Jodi's ass cheek. She pulled hard and forcefully and Jodi met her with another solid thrust, driving Eve's petite body against the surface.

She tugged at Jodi's shirt while bucking against her. "Get this shirt off. I'm dying to get my tongue on that brick-hard tummy."

Jodi arched away long enough to drag the shirt over her head. When she looked back to Eve, she lost herself in those fuck-me eyes. She could feel her wall of reserve tremble as Eve thrust and ground, her sights trained on Jodi's lips.

Jodi slammed against her pussy just as her head moved forward.

Eve whipped back, a guttural groan sliding from her mouth. "Shit, yes!"

Jodi dipped her tongue in the hollow of Eve's throat, then sucked the indention. She was coming apart, and it felt incredible. Her body was a bundle of flared nerves, stinging as the heat careened through her veins.

The phone was one thing, but having those moans rushing against her face, ringing against her ears, was quite another. Eve was going to rip her apart, one sweet cry after another.

She tightened her grip around Eve's ass and legs, then stumbled for the bedroom, needing flesh against her tongue, and something soft for Eve to thrash against.

Eve was fisting her hair, her lips locked against Jodi's neck, when they landed in a heap in the middle of the bed. She looked up at Jodi, her eyes downcast, her breath harsh puffs.

Before she knew Eve had moved, her lips were against Jodi's.

Jodi expelled a moan, struggling for control, losing the battle before it ever began, and then slipped her tongue into Eve's mouth.

She was vaguely aware of one of them moaning as she pulled Eve tighter against her body, their tongues invading and exploring and owning.

When Eve hummed against her mouth, it was all Jodi could do to hang on to her sanity. She massaged and kneaded the muscles down Jodi's side and back then palmed her ass cheeks again, driving Jodi between her legs.

When she pulled free of the kiss, Jodi felt empty, lost without the connection. Eve pushed against her shoulders until Jodi rolled onto her back. Eve followed and straddled her. With a needy expression, Eve lifted her T-shirt over her head, staring down over Jodi like she was already deep inside her. With a flick of her wrist, she tossed the material off the bed, then ground down hard against Jodi, her lips slightly parting, her eyes focused. "You sure there's no girlfriend I should worry about storming home to catch you? I'm not in the mood to share tonight."

Not that Eve cared about a better half at this particular moment in time. Hell, she'd be tempted to invite the bitch to join them. No fucking way was she going to pass up an opportunity with this gorgeous stallion between her thighs, with a woman she only dreamed up in her mind, who was in the flesh for her taking right now.

Jodi palmed her thighs and drove upward. "No girlfriends. I'm all yours."

Eve was relieved, yet not relieved at all. Jodi was handsome, a gentleman, had a steady job and a killer condo, yet she hadn't been snatched out of the sea of sexy women? Eve's red flag jerked to attention. Maybe she was a womanizer. Or an abuser? Maybe she was a bad fuck. She said a silent prayer the latter wasn't true. She'd seen it happen before, sadly, firsthand. There was nothing more draining than working up for the best fuck of all times only to have reality ripped from your conscious with a lousy lay.

The way Jodi was driving against her, grinding her pussy into a hot flame, she was doubtful this night would end any other way than with Jodi's name flying past her lips.

Eve circled her hips and looked down at the grooved stomach muscles between the vee of her legs. Dear God, only in her mind had a woman borne such detailed cuts. She fingered lightly across one, and then reversed across another.

"I thought you were going to lick those."

"That and more." Eve licked her lips, wanting Jodi inside her, pumping and slamming into her. "But first, you're going to get me naked."

"Is that right?" Jodi whipped Eve onto her back, then fingered the edge of her bra before pulling the lace down to expose a dark nipple.

The sight of Jodi soaking in her naked flesh had goose bumps trailing across Eve's skin. Her nipple peaked tighter under that penetrating stare.

"What say we work our way to that? Slowly." Jodi ducked and swiped the tip of her tongue across her pebbled creation.

Eve arched as fire traveled in branches down her body. Her clit pulsed and she ground against Jodi's leg to ease the burn. Jodi clamped her teeth around her nipple and Eve froze save for a shocked gasp. Tingles sparked across her crotch as Jodi gave a slight tug.

"Don't move until I say move."

Her tongue flicked across Eve's nipple and cream pooled against Eve's thong. God save her soul, that domination made her so fucking horny. She wanted Jodi to bite down hard, to leave teeth marks in her flesh, to flip her over and fuck her until she begged to come.

Until now, only Lexi had gotten away with such power and only because Eve willingly handed her control, leaving her own power aside for those glorious phone calls. But never in person. In her bed, she was still in control. And right now, someone strong, sexy, and fuckable was going to rip it away without daring to ask permission.

"Did that make you horny, Eve?" Jodi rewarded the other breast with as much attention as the first and Eve moaned, yet not daring to press herself around that leg again. Her insides clenched and burned as she struggled not to pump her hips. "You like being controlled?"

Eve fisted her hands when Jodi closed her teeth over her nipple and tugged. When she pulled harder, Eve sucked in a breath, realizing Jodi was demanding an answer. "No."

Jodi increased the pressure and Eve's nipple stung with splendid heat. She arched and released a soft cry.

"Don't move." Jodi's teeth clamped tighter.

Son of a bitch, this woman was serious about her rules. Fuck if it wasn't making Eve a suffering wet mess. She lowered her hips and willed them not to move again though the pressure on her nipple didn't ease.

Jodi knew she was lying.

Eve clenched her fists tighter, fighting for control of her body. "Yes! I like it. You happy?"

Jodi released her nipple, then wiggled between her legs, wanting to eat Eve alive, wanting inside her, all the way to the fucking core of her. No other woman had ever made such dizzy emotions jumble inside her before. One minute she wanted to stretch out across Eve and make intimate love to her, the next she wanted to rip her apart like a werewolf and fuck her until she passed out. But the fact that Eve sought Lexi's demands, tossing her power away so freely over the line, left Jodi with no other choice but to give her what she knew she wanted. Her power stripped.

"I know what you want, Eve." Jodi snagged open the rivet of Eve's jeans, then leaned down to lick her tanned, flat stomach just above a baby blue thong.

"What? Tell me." Eve trembled and her fist opened and closed as she raked her nails along the comforter.

Jodi smiled and sucked at her skin before licking a wet path down the faint goodie trail leading into her panties. Eve was struggling. And Jodi would be damned if she showed Eve her own personal fight, how she was crumbling with this sweet skin against her tongue. "You want me to control you. And fuck you."

"Yes, please. The last first. I'm burning to hell and back."

"If I fucked you first, what fun would I have dominating you?" Jodi tugged her jeans and thong down around her ass, then thought better of it and pushed them all the way down until they caught and locked around those piss-poor boots. With one final glance at those pleading eyes, she dipped her tongue into the alcove of Eve's parted thighs, inhaling her scent of arousal.

Lights burst behind her closed lids when Eve cried out. That sound, so raw and unbridled, sent a current of electricity surging through her body.

"Jodi, please just fuck me. Now! We can play the control game later, I swear." Eve thrust against her face and tangled her fingers into Jodi's hair.

Jodi whipped upright, wanting to scold her like she would over the phone for disobeying. But she wasn't on a phone this time. This time, Eve was beneath her, needing her much more than she'd ever needed Lexi. And what a fucking sight she was—her nipples proud and upright, her lean stomach tight with each ragged breath, the exact image she'd seen in her mind when she wanted Eve looking like a two-bit slut.

Eve's gaze dipped to Jodi's covered breasts, to her stomach, then flashed back to her face. "Are you gonna fuck me or memorize me?"

"Oh, I'm gonna fuck you all right." Jodi straddled one of her legs and teased her slit, recalling a little secret Eve had shared with her during one of their more intimate nights after Eve had come, when she was in her drained moment. Eve expelled a sigh and her lids fluttered but didn't close. "But first, I'm going to play...and tease."

Jodi slicked her finger through juices, teasing to the first knuckle. She added another and did the same, slowly pushing inside her to the second knuckle.

"Oh, yes. Play. Play all you want." Eve's body was tight with anticipation, her knees spread wide, her back arched, and those dark nipples straining against the air.

Jodi entered to the palm in a single thrust. When Eve cried out and whipped her head back, Jodi had to close her eyes. She ground down against Eve's leg, her pussy a candescent ball of fire, her mind consumed with the sound of that cry. How much sweeter, purer, it sounded penetrating her bedroom.

So many nights, so many calls, and so many times, she'd been accosted by that very sound of Eve screaming helplessly, with Jodi unable to touch, or feel, or taste, fighting against the need to join Eve in her erotic moment. A reaction she'd never had to a client.

Now she could. Now she could strip them both naked and fall against her heated flesh. She could take her, violate her, over and over, in every way possible. Eve wanted her, wanted Jodi. Lexi wasn't at play here. She wasn't in charge tonight. After this night, she was going to make sure it was Jodi's face she saw when Lexi coaxed her to a back-arching orgasm.

Jodi opened her eyes and concentrated on Eve's silky smooth skin, on everything she wanted to do before their night was through. Eve's confession came back to mind—that she'd never had an internal orgasm.

She wanted to be Eve's first. She would be her first.

With her thoughts overwhelming, she withdrew to the first knuckle.

Eve relaxed, focused, then reached for Jodi. "There are so many ways to play, to make me come. We can try them all."

Jodi pushed her back down and warned with a cocked brow.

"I intend to do just that." Jodi curled a finger up against the spongy surface before Eve could disobey further and stroked with a practiced come-hither motion. Eve sucked in a breath, her eyes wide before fluttering closed. With her other hand, Jodi pressed down against her pelvic bone and thrust her working finger more forcefully.

The motion set Eve on fire, yet trailing close behind was cold and numb. She wasn't even sure she had feeling in her toes and fingers anymore. The only thing she could concentrate on was the incredible sensation consuming her body, her mind, of Jodi's determined face, of that finger stroking her somewhere she'd obviously never been touched before—a secret she'd only shared with one person. Lexi.

She slung her head back when Jodi thumbed her clit. Why the hell was she thinking about a phone voice when a real live woman was on her knees between her thighs, doing something Godly to her body?

Jodi pressed harder and added another finger to the majestic strokes, doubling the sensations. Eve dug her head to the side, fisting the comforter. The pressure in her pussy was almost unbearable, gloriously unbearable. When Jodi stroked faster, she grabbed the iron bars on the headboard for leverage.

Jodi ground down against her leg again and moaned. Eve moaned too at the sight of her crotch bearing down on her. This was making Jodi horny, and Eve was without power to assist her. Right now, every muscle in her body was tight as a fist.

Another wave of heat and bliss washed over her and her pussy clenched down hard around Jodi's fingers. Eve slung her head to the other side and yanked at the bars.

"Jesus, what are you doing to me? I'm…I'm…fuck!" The pressure increased and Eve instinctively clamped her legs together, only to find a solid obstacle in her way—Jodi's muscled thigh.

Jodi ground against Eve's leg, faster, harder. "Let it go, Eve."

Eve bucked, instantly scared to release whatever was threatening to burst. It was unlike anything she'd ever felt—impelling, rushing, pushing, torturous almost, yet not at all.

Jodi stroked harder and Eve practically bent the bars in half with a brutal tug. Her arms were numb, her fingers far past that point, yet she couldn't let go, couldn't release the hold on anything solid.

When Jodi's hips bucked down hard against her leg and her breath hitched, Eve opened her eyes. Jodi's face was upturned, teeth ground tight, the muscles in her neck corded and stressed.

Jodi released a deep, throaty moan. It was the most erotic thing she'd ever seen. Jodi coming.

"Fuck." Jodi spasmed while her hips pumped and circled in demanding drives.

Eve couldn't look away, enthralled with the hunk coming against her, on her. Then Jodi opened her eyes and trapped Eve in that stable stare. The way she was looking at her, like she knew her, really knew her, her heart, her soul, her fantasies and her deep, dark secrets.

Jodi's fingers surged upward and Eve cried out in shock. She lost her grip on the ravishing pressure and came in a blinding brilliance of light.

"Oh God! Oh, fuck! Oh, my fucking God!" Her muscles spasmed around Jodi's fingers tight and fast and hard, closing her insides in painful clamps, only to release the vise as quickly as it tightened.

She knew she was screaming, knew she was bucking and thrashing like a wild mustang, knew she was yanking the bars like a prisoner. But sweet glorious heavens, she was coming so fucking hard.

And then Jodi was between her legs, pinning her thighs apart, lapping and sucking her clit, hungry and moaning, drinking every drop of her, forcing those fingers deep. Eve's body quivered and pumped while she mewled and thrashed, while her pussy strangled long fingers.

Just when she thought the spasms were going to ignite again, her body jerked forward, then she fell back in a boneless heap on the pillow, sucking in heaping gulps of air until her lungs were satisfied. Jodi climbed up her body and smoothed feather-soft kisses along her chin and throat, her forearms cocooning Eve on either side. Eve didn't even have the energy to smile at her, not even a simple pleasure-filled moan. She felt drained and empty, yet fulfilled and satisfied beyond recognition.

"You okay?" Jodi stroked damp strands of hair away from Eve's face.

"Mmmm." Eve shook her head but wasn't sure the gesture went past the mental action. She wasn't sure if she could move any part of her body at all, and right now, she didn't want to. Lying here, with those soft lips coaxing wet heat against her skin, with feeling prickling back to life along her limbs, was all she wanted.

She didn't care about work or designs. Or the fact that she was half-dressed with all vital parts exposed to Jodi. She didn't care about anything else but the right here and now, the sexy woman hovering over her, who'd just fucked the get up and go right out of her.

When Jodi withdrew and her weight left the bed, Eve groaned. As lethargic as she was, she wasn't ready to leave this bed, or Jodi's side.

"Time to get you completely naked. We've only gotten started."

CHAPTER TEN

Jodi pulled Eve's boots and jeans off her feet. The pliable leather landed on the floor with a soft thud. She could still taste Eve's sweet come on her lips. Her gut ached. Her soul was in shambles. Eve's cries and screams had ripped at her until there was nothing left but sorrow. Sorrow that she would have to say good-bye to her. Sorrow that Eve would never know the real Jodi. Or the real Lexi. Sorrow that she was ashamed for once in her life of the real life she led.

This whole night was nothing more than a fantasy, a fantasy come true. She knew the experience was going to change her forever, and she wasn't sure how she felt about it.

Eve moaned, still boneless against the mattress. God, those sounds. That body rocking against her face, those angelic cries. She was never going to forget them.

With a sigh, she kicked out of her jeans and briefs, then pulled her sports bra over her head. She wasn't done with Eve. Wasn't sure she could ever be, though in less than a week she'd have no other choice but to be. That was then. Tonight she was going to seduce Eve, caressing every sleek inch of her, and when this week was over, she'd swallow the consequences of her actions.

Jodi made her way to the nightstand and withdrew her dildo. The very one that matched Eve's. She tightened the straps in place, then crawled across the bed.

Once she'd slid against Eve's side, spooning against her delicate skin, she fingered her lower lip for several seconds and ducked for a kiss. She knew she shouldn't. It was too personal, too close. She shouldn't want or need to kiss her. But she did.

Her ironclad rules faded as Eve opened for her, exploring her mouth, a soft whimper escaping as Jodi slipped her tongue inside.

Eve's arm fell around Jodi's neck. Jodi flipped the bra catch between her breasts and pushed the straps down her arms.

She urged Eve onto her side and ducked to the crook of her neck, inhaling her sweet aroma, then pulled one leg up and over her hip.

Eve tensed and Jodi palmed her breasts, teasing pebbled nipples. When Eve relaxed, Jodi fanned her hand open and stroked across her rib cage, over that smooth, trim belly, down between her legs, until her fingers dipped between wet folds.

Eve dug her ass into Jodi and released a soft cry. "Jesus, Jodi. I can't do that again," she protested, though her body language said differently as her hips shifted forward, then backward.

Jodi reached back until she found the head of the dildo. "You can. I promise." She kissed Eve's cheek while she guided the tip inside her.

Eve bowed backward, slowly driving her pussy down over the dildo. "I'm going to be worthless tomorrow. Roger is going to have a coronary. And Khandi is going to have a field day trying to figure out what got me this way."

Jodi laughed and pushed deeper. "You can thank me later."

Eve pushed back. "Who said I was going to thank you at all?"

Jodi flicked her clit. Eve hissed between clenched teeth. "Haven't you ever heard actions speak louder than words?" She flicked harder and Eve pressed into her hand. "Your actions are screaming thank you, thank you, thank you right this very second."

"Shit, it is. Keep doing that. Please!" Eve's backward thrusts kicked up speed. Soon she was driving herself over the dildo, her muscles tight, and her pussy hot and slick.

Jodi took Eve's hand and led it down between her legs. "Make yourself come, Eve."

Without hesitation, Eve began to flick. Her hips surged, her middle finger circled, and her stomach muscles tightened. Jodi would see this image with every phone call—Eve lost in the throes of passion.

The tickler at the base dug against Jodi's clit with every thrust, pushing her orgasm to the edge. Or rather, Eve's cries were. The sound was driving her stupid. She wondered if those cries alone could make her come. Lord knew they made her wet much faster—so close to her, in her arms, in her grasp, in her fucking bed.

"Jodi, shit! I'm coming! Oooh." Eve trembled and Jodi hooked her arm beneath her leg and lifted it higher, driving into her with deep, powerful thrusts.

Eve's high pitch whine jerked Jodi's orgasm to the surface, then cascaded over her in ragged clenches. She clung to Eve, bucking toward her, against her, inside her, until they both sagged.

For several long minutes, she cradled Eve close to her body, drunk on adrenaline, drunk with the scent of Eve, with her sounds.

Drunk in lust.

❖

Eve opened her eyes to find a window covered by sheer white drapes. The sun was bright, casting rays of light through the open slit.

With a start, she remembered where she was.

She was in Jodi's bed. That was her arm limp across Eve's hip. That was her other arm beneath her head. And that was her tight stomach pressed against Eve's back and her legs tangled with Eve's.

It was the sexy prop assistant who'd fucked her into a semi-coma, not once, but three times throughout the night. How had she done that? She was like an orgasm pro, making Eve scream out even on the last orgasm, when she was positive it couldn't be done. She had no idea what number orgasm that had been, possibly ten, though the soreness seeping into her bones laughed at her. Was it more like twenty? Was that number even possible?

If only Lexi had answered her phone, maybe her sexual hunger would have been at bay when she spotted Jodi perched on the curb like a barbarian goddess.

Dammit, she couldn't help herself. Jodi was delicious, and right now Eve didn't have a single regret. Hell, how could she after that night of hair-pulling orgasms? No harm done. Just two grown women having a little unadulterated sex. Okay, so that was more than a little, but she'd deserved every clench of it. After this week, she'd be back to business as usual, with Jodi nothing more than a fond memory. But this week she was going to enjoy Jodi playing her body like a harmonica.

Eve closed her eyes and soaked in the heat from the morning sun, the world coming to life. She was so rested it was scary, though slight panic nipped at her conscious. She hadn't stayed overnight with another woman in so long, and now here she'd done just that with a virtual stranger.

It helped that Jodi was nail-bitingly sexy. And the things she'd done to Eve's body had verged on miraculous, yet were uncannily familiar in a super-strange kind of way. As if Jodi knew exactly what Eve had wanted, what she wouldn't allow, what she was dying to try. Like she already knew the answers.

Eve allowed herself fifteen more minutes in the confinement of Jodi's heated skin, of listening to her steady breathing against her back, and the comfort of those strong arms protecting her. She was late for work. That was okay. Hell, half her staff was probably thrilled she wasn't on set yet. Less of her mouth they had to hear.

Khandi would make sure things ran smoothly without her, and as much as Roger hated getting off schedule, he'd bend hell to keep that tight itinerary. She wasn't missing anything vital this morning, just final adjustments before the real hell began. Tomorrow was her last day to put everything together. The day after that, her creations would fill the runway.

The thought gave her a rush, the exact thing she needed to roll over and face Jodi.

Jodi opened her eyes to find Eve looking up at her. She smiled. Eve was still there, in her bed, in her arms, a lazy smile playing across those pouty morning lips. She drew Eve to her body, not ready to release their skin-on-skin contact. "Morning, sexy."

"We're late for work."

"I'm never late for work. Remember?" Jodi snuggled into the crook of her neck. "Amelia is the coolest boss in the world."

"Ah. I see. Well, seeing as I am the boss, I'm ordering myself out of this bed." Eve attempted to roll over but Jodi grabbed her waist and rolled on top of her. She kneed her legs apart and Eve automatically locked her between her thighs, her hips instinctively surging forward.

Jodi kissed her, hard, forcing her crotch against that sweet pussy. She was positive she was addicted to Eve, to her scent, to her fucking sounds.

"God, Jodi, stop. You're a sex maniac." Eve pushed against her. "I really, really, really can't do this."

Jodi sucked at the indention in her throat, then moved lower to curl her tongue around an awakening nipple. "Sure you can. There's one position we didn't get to."

Eve arched into her mouth. "That can't be possible." She stroked her fingers into Jodi's hair. "I came in every position humanly possible last night. Twice. Or was it more? I lost count."

"Not this one." Jodi crawled between her thighs and shoved her legs apart, locking them in place against the bed with brute strength. With a wicked smile, she lowered her face.

Eve's clit bobbed and swelled against her tongue. Jodi slurped at her, swiping her tongue along her wet slit, teasing and flicking, drawing Eve into those angelic cries before she latched on. She tightened her grip on Eve's legs to give the minor sensation of shackles, fearful she'd leave bruises yet hoping she did, and then Eve slammed her fists against the bed and her pussy started pulsing against Jodi's mouth.

"Godohgodohohohohohgodoh...shit!" Eve thrashed her head from side to side, her hips locked in place by Jodi's grasp.

Jodi screwed her eyes tight. No matter how hard she tried, the sound of Eve coming would always jolt her to the core. The sound was addictive. Downright fucking addictive.

She flicked for several more seconds and just when Eve slacked, she drove her tongue inside those quivering muscles.

"Fuck, Jodi!" Eve practically rose to a sitting position before she fell back and jerked at the sheets.

Long minutes passed while Eve convulsed against her mouth, around her tongue, then she was motionless.

Jodi let loose her hold and checked for bruises on those delicate legs. She smiled at the faint red finger marks. Every step that Eve took today, she was going to remember this night, this morning. She climbed up Eve's body to kiss her cheek.

"Get away from me." Eve chuckled. "And don't touch me. You're trying to kill me. I know it."

Jodi lay beside her. "I do try."

"That you do." Eve opened her eyes, a serious expression on her face. "Thanks for a great night."

Jodi cringed. She couldn't count the times she'd heard those exact words, followed by the deliverance of a fat envelope. The words coming from Eve made her feel cheap for some reason, or rather, cheated. She'd put everything she had into their night only to have the identical words flow from her mouth.

"I thought you didn't give out thank-yous."

"I don't, normally. Consider yourself special." With a quick peck on the lips, Eve rolled off the bed and went in search of her clothes. She found her thong and warned Jodi with a stern glare. "Don't think about getting off that bed. I seriously have to get to work."

"Too late. I'm struggling with the thought right now." She moved to the end of the bed to tease.

Eve flew to each piece of clothing, watching Jodi with a wary eye, and all too soon, she'd covered that petite body with clothes, just the way she'd entered the apartment. She was a fascinating creature, unlike the Eve that came screaming over the wire. Flirty and fun out of her realm of fashion, all business and gung-ho once she stepped inside it. Those characteristics fascinated Jodi while Eve walked toward the door. She'd never met anyone like her. She was different. Jodi had known that from the second she'd answered her private line and found Eve's hesitant voice on the other end.

Without looking back, Eve reached for the knob and cracked opened the door. The action galvanized Jodi off the bed. She reached over Eve's shoulder and slammed the door shut.

"Leaving without a good-bye kiss?" Jodi nuzzled her neck and pressed against her.

"Hell, yes. I'm not a pussy to admit you make me weak." Eve turned around and grinned.

Jodi liked those smiling eyes, the way her lips curled up at the corners. She lowered her mouth to Eve and slicked her tongue inside.

Eve expelled a sigh and her arms dropped around Jodi's shoulder. She palmed the back of Jodi's neck and deepened the kiss, her tongue swiping against Jodi's, her body responding in slow grinds against Jodi.

She pushed hard, and Jodi stumbled back. "Stop it! No more. The studio is going to fall down around my ears if I don't get to work."

Before Jodi could respond, she was out the bedroom door, followed closely by the closing of the front door.

Jodi chuckled. "Run, Eve, but you'll be back."

Eve would always be back. She was addicted to a fantasy, and Jodi—Lexi—was her optical illusion.

❖

Eve raced into her hotel suite, shedding clothes as she raced for the shower. Her body ached with tender pain from her ankles all the way to back of her neck. Hypersensitive in every place Jodi had touched her or fucked her. God, it hurt so good. How she wished she could keep the memory intact and just curl up and sleep. And fantasize about Jodi inside her, fucking her, making her come like no one before. Was being fucked into a boneless husk of woman a good enough reason to call in sick? Wouldn't Khandi have a field day with that excuse?

She ducked under the hot spray and showered as quickly as possible, lingering lightly over all those acute places where Jodi had coaxed her to yet another quenching orgasm.

How could a complete stranger know so much about her, about her body, where and what would make her scream? It was eerie, yet calming. No other woman had taken such initiative, or such care. Hell, no other woman had cared to listen long enough for Eve to tell her such personal things.

Well, one had. Lexi. Lexi knew her fantasies, where she liked to be touched, caressed. Yet Lexi didn't count. She was nothing more than a phone voice, a sponge for someone's perverted thoughts. It was her job to listen, her job to help Eve reach some of those intimate needs. She was damn sure paying enough for her ears. And for her demands.

"Damn!" Eve rinsed her hair and cut off the water. "What the hell is wrong with me?"

She stepped out of the shower and brushed her hand across the fog-filled mirror to see her reflection. What kind of woman was addicted to a phone voice? Was it because Lexi listened? Because she faked caring? Because she seemed to memorize everything Eve confessed, using the information to good effect through every phone call? Because Eve's money paid her bills?

Of course. She was a pro. A fucking sex phone operator. No doubt she had a file for every client, a simple task to sift through the folders to find her personal notes on each.

Where's my file on Eve? Oh, here it is. Yes, oh my, Eve likes to be fucked with a dildo, likes a single finger fucking her ass just before she comes. Now I have the right caller. I almost got her mixed up with Mitzy. Yikes.

Eve huffed at her reflection. She needed to stop this nonsense, this ridiculous behavior. She didn't need Lexi to give her satisfaction. Her life was fulfilled and enriched by a wonderful career, and if she needed to get her hands on a woman that badly, the nearest lesbian bar held plenty of women who'd be willing and able to supply what her body craved. Hell, Lexi wasn't giving her those things anyway. She was giving them to herself while Lexi guided the way, talked her through every motion.

What a freak she was. What an absolute caprice.

Lexi's British accent spun through her mind and she gripped the counter for support. What the hell was she thinking? Lexi was perfect. She was perfect for Eve and her rushed life. No matter where she went, or what she was doing, Lexi was always only a phone call away. It was the most unflawed relationship she'd ever had.

She could fight facts all she wanted, but she knew the truth. She was addicted to Lexi.

Dressed and ready for work, Eve grabbed her purse and headed out the door. She dug for her phone and found six missed calls from Khandi. She was probably anxious to hear about Eve's night.

Not that she could share those intimate moments so quickly. Just a few more days to keep them to herself, enough time to get back home, back to the real world, and she'd give Khandi every little juicy tidbit. But for now, they were all hers to shelter. God knew the thoughts were going to keep her wet all damn day.

She dialed Khandi's number to let her know she wasn't a victim at the bottom of the Thames.

"I'm pissed at you."

Eve smiled. "What else is new? You're always pissed at me."

"Where the hell were you all night? I was worried sick."

Eve stepped out of the elevator and walked across the foyer. "Get back to work, Ms. Nosy. See you in a few."

She disconnected the line and stepped out into the bright sunshine.

It wasn't raining, though she had her umbrella armed and ready and a hunk of burning desire on her mind.

She wanted to do it again. Every blissful part of it.

CHAPTER ELEVEN

Jodi crept in the side door and paused to assess the scene. The loud voices and rushed surroundings had become normal rather than a distraction. She spotted Amelia inside their little makeshift area and eased hesitantly through the groups of people absorbed in their own world. If there was anyone who would catch on to the fact that the boss was missing, along with Jodi, it was Amelia.

When Amelia turned a deadly expression her way, she thought twice about staying. Hell, she wanted to run. "Tell me you didn't do her."

"Do her?" Jodi cocked a brow. She couldn't lie. Amelia could smell a fib a mile away. "Remind me, do we *do* them in middle or high school? Between *will you go with me* and *can I do you* I totally forget."

Amelia waved an X-Acto knife at her and Jodi took a step back, keeping a smile on her face though she wasn't positive Amelia wouldn't swing the knife at her. God, she looked pissed.

"You're playing with fire, Jodi. Not just your fire, it's mine too. You're fucking with my career!"

Jodi knew she was right, knew she was being self-centered, if not self-destructive.

"Calm down, Mel. It wasn't like that." Jodi gave her a charming smile and batted her eyes.

"Yeah, like you've ever just walked a girl home." Amelia pointed the unopened knife toward Jodi. "And don't call me Mel when I'm on the verge of being pissed." A smile teetered on her lips and she lifted her head higher in an attempt to look more serious.

"Are you done? Feel better now?" Jodi grinned.

Amelia shook her head and crossed her arms. "No, I don't feel better. Under normal circumstances, I'd say fuck whoever you want. But this is different. I really want this job. If she finds out about the real you, I can kiss this job good-bye."

Jodi stepped toward her. "Mel, trust me, that won't happen. The Eve I know behind the scenes would probably hire you just for knowing me." She looked around the room. "The bitch who takes over during working hours, well, I'm not so sure about her evil twin. What I do know is both of them will be in a much better mood today."

Amelia rolled her eyes. "You're fucking with my career no matter which twin you're charming."

"Ah, is that we're calling it nowadays?"

Amelia's eyes narrowed. "Fuck you, Jodi." She stormed away and knelt to arrange chrome-colored twigs.

Jodi's heart ached. Amelia was the only important thing in her life, the only thing that truly mattered. She took Jodi as she was, and though she tossed her two cents around like Jodi was her personal wishing well, Jodi's well-being was the only thing that mattered to Amelia.

How could she fuck with that? How could she step over those boundaries to harm Amelia's newfound career, just when it was taking off at warp speed? What a sap she was, and how she wished she could regret last night, and the wee hours of the morning. She couldn't, not even for Amelia. She hated herself more for that. For putting someone else above the only steady and stable person in her life.

Jodi forked her fingers through her hair and approached Amelia. "I'm sorry, Amelia. I never could have seen this coming, for her to show up like that. I'll stay away from her if that's what you want." She waited for a reaction, terrified Amelia would demand she never set eyes on Eve again.

She wasn't sure she could. Wasn't sure how she could.

Amelia looked up from her kneeled position, thankfully, a smile dancing on her lips, while trying to maintain her serious expression. "You're so full of shit."

Jodi hung her head. "I know, but it sure sounded good. For you, I would try damn hard, though. Does that count?"

Amelia nodded and chuckled. "Straight or not, I would have fucked her without thinking twice about your slack ass either."

Jodi burst out laughing and the tension of the moment washed away.

"But don't you dare think for a second you're off the hook. I'm still pissed at you. And if she finds out before this week is over, there will be a fresh new body floating in the Thames. Got it?"

"Loud and clear."

Now she'd have to struggle to keep her gaze off Eve all day. Only a few more days and Eve would fly back to her life across the map, and hopefully, surely, they'd continue their phone sex sessions. At least Jodi could still look forward to the calls. But then what? Eve would never know that she'd been in Lexi's bed, whispering the first part of Jodi's birth name, Jodesy Alexis. She'd never know that the woman she fucked in London was the Lexi she sought for sexual comfort a few nights a week over the wire.

The conclusion saddened Jodi. Eve wanted the fantasy. She wanted Lexi. She wanted the fantasy of Lexi to fit into her perfect chaotic life. Eve didn't have room for real relationships. Hell, maybe she worked ungodly hours for that very reason, to keep unnecessary blotches out of her otherwise spic-and-span world.

Jodi knew deep down, she should stay far, far away from Eve. She also knew she couldn't and wouldn't. That flame they'd kindled over a phone had ruptured into a working wildfire with the mere strut across the studio on once classy boots.

As if she'd mentally summoned her, Eve appeared from one of the private rooms, a trail of employees in her wake, their voices competing with one another to be heard first. Eve flicked a cool glance down Jodi's body without a single twitch of an eyebrow. Man, did she ever know how to hide desire. Or rather, she hoped Eve was doing a grand job of masking it. Was it possible to go from screaming someone's name to never letting it escape her mouth again?

Jodi prayed she would stop to make conversation, then prayed she wouldn't.

Eve turned in their direction, and Jodi's insides clamped down tight. Her posse never lost stride with her rushed steps. She stopped in front of Jodi, her expression cold and uncaring. "Amelia. Jodi. Good morning."

Amelia stood, her face frozen in a fake smile. "Yes, good morning, Eve. I'm just adding a few final touches."

"Great. I'm thrilled with the props. You two have done a great job."

Khandi shoved a clipboard into Eve's hand, and Eve looked away to study the page, then signed it.

Jodi begged for Eve to look at her the way she had this morning, for those eyes to mentally undress her.

"Thank you," Amelia said.

"I wanted to extend an invitation to the finale dinner Friday night. Both of you." She glanced at Jodi, not even the slightest flicker of sexual longing.

Jodi's heart drilled against her rib cage. She'd never met anyone who could transform like that—from an animal in bed to an ice princess at work, all within hours of coming, only hours after bellowing Jodi's name. She wasn't sure how she felt about it, or why it bothered her.

Amelia nodded. "Absolutely. We'd love to attend. Thank you."

Eve's BlackBerry chirped by her side. She withdrew it, read the message, and then handed the phone to Khandi. "Have her meet us in the conference room in ten. If she's late, she's out of luck. I have an interview in thirty."

She turned back to Amelia. "When do you predict you'll be complete?"

"Say, two, maybe three hours?" Amelia fidgeted with the knife still clamped tight in her grasp.

Eve pointed to Roger, who promptly punched buttons on his PDA.

"I'll be back then to give my final approval. Good day, ladies." Eve turned and walked away without a second glance back.

Jodi stood in shocked silence as Eve's posse folded around her. She felt violated, used. She turned to find Amelia watching her, her eyes soft and filled with sorrow and a little mockery.

"You call that a better mood? Man, you're losing your touch, Connelly." Amelia snickered, then squatted to gather up the twigs.

Jodi walked around Amelia to the final prop, wishing Eve could have at least given her a tiny wink or a lingering glance. Anything would have been better than complete dismissal.

Four hours later, Jodi had managed to stop looking for Eve and wishing for the sight of her. Every time Eve had passed her, she'd barely glanced in Jodi's direction, and even then, it was like she was looking over her, around her, right through her.

It was downright disturbing and left something hollow in the pit of her stomach. Eve had business to attend to, had been swarmed with a crew stumbling to keep up with her all morning, but a glance, a tiny wiggle of an eyebrow, a sparkle of acknowledgment in her eyes, anything!

Amelia stood back from the finished prop, wiped a thin film of sweat and loose hair from her face, and sighed. "Finally. Done." She looked over to Jodi. "You hungry?"

Jodi shook her head. Fact was, she hadn't thought about food all day. Eve, yes, but not food. Unless Eve was the food, then yes, she'd thought of nothing else.

"Want me to bring you back a sandwich? Ham and Swiss?" Amelia propped her hands on her hips, a true indication she was uneasy about something.

"Maybe I should go grab lunch. The ice queen should be back soon to inspect."

Amelia tilted her head back and studied Jodi with narrowed eyes. "The ice queen is here now."

Jodi stiffened with Eve's words, a lump lodged in her throat. Amelia whipped around so fast her hair struck Jodi in the face.

"Eve, hi, I'm—" Amelia stammered and Jodi wanted to fold herself into the nearest prop. Fuck! Her and her big mouth. And her bruised ego.

Eve dismissed her quickly by stepping around both her and Jodi. As she knelt by the props, Amelia stomped down hard on Jodi's loafer.

Jodi sucked in a yelp and looked over to find Khandi staring at her, a devious smile plastered on her mouth. What the hell was up with that woman? This wasn't the first time she'd caught her curious eyes. Or were those knowing eyes? And now she was making up things to worry over.

Either way, she was playing with fire. She had been from the second she agreed to assist Amelia, from the second she'd heard Eve say her own name. She could have never foreseen Eve being the boss, "the" voice on the other end of the phone. But from the second she recognized that sound, she should have blown this joint and saved Amelia from doomsday.

If she didn't get a permanent spot in Eve's fashion world, Jodi would only have herself to blame.

And now it was too late. She'd fucked the boss and loved every minute of it. She was going to do it again before Eve left the country. And she was going to enjoy every minute of those screams.

God, she was totally fucked.

"These are incredible, Amelia. I'm in awe of your work." Eve rose and looked for Roger, who quickly darted to her side. "Call transport to get these packaged."

Roger nodded once, punched buttons on his PDA, then withdrew his cell phone before stepping away.

The act turned Jodi on—how Eve didn't even have to snap her fingers before people jumped to attention. Large and in charge. Every second of every day.

No wonder she wanted Lexi in her life. Lexi took away the stress and her control. Lexi gave her what her body craved from far, far away.

Eve moved back from the props and turned to Jodi, a hint of curiosity sparkling in her eyes.

Jodi stuffed her hands in her pockets and looked away, heat crawling across her crotch like hot metal talons.

"Eve, I was just about to make a run for sandwiches. Would you like anything?" Amelia asked calmly, as if Jodi hadn't just called her new boss a bitch, in a nice way.

"Thanks, but Khandi was just about to round us up some lunch."

"I was?" Khandi stiffened.

"Yes, you were." Eve gave her a scolding glance and Khandi rolled her eyes before scurrying away. Roger took the hint and followed her.

Amelia looked between Jodi and Eve. "Okay, then. I'll be back soon." She gave Jodi a final glance, as if waiting for Jodi to change her mind, almost pleading for her to change her mind.

She finally turned and walked away.

"Follow me, Jodi." Eve stepped around Jodi and strode off.

Like a puppet controlled by the puppet master, Jodi willingly followed her. She would follow her right into Armageddon if that's where that sexy ass led her.

Again, an unfamiliar emotion. One she liked, though she knew she shouldn't.

They continued their hurried steps down a long hallway, past varied groups of people engrossed in conversation. Eve made a sharp right then another sharp left, into a section of the studio Jodi was sure was off-limits to even the fashion crews.

When Eve came to a sudden stop, Jodi practically barreled into her. Eve looked over both shoulders, then fisted her hand into Jodi's T-shirt and tugged her inside an office. With a swift kick, she slammed the door and locked it.

She walked around Jodi as if she wasn't even in the room and approached a long oak desk. "Think you can latch that hot mouth around this ice queen's pussy?"

Jodi swallowed. "I think I can handle that task."

Eve turned her back to the desk while Jodi stood frozen. She kicked off her boots, tugged down a pair of ripped-knee jeans, then pulled herself onto the desk. "Can you do it now?"

Jodi started across the room on quivery legs, damned if she was going to show Eve how unstable she was. She approached her and palmed the tops of her legs, then slammed her thighs apart. "Earn it."

"Excuse me?" Eve reached for her, but Jodi leaned out of her grasp and dipped a single finger against her slit, dragging her finger through her juice, then higher to tease her clit.

"Earn this hot mouth." Jodi removed her hand, snagged open her jeans and shoved them down to her knees. "Make me come, Eve. With *your* mouth."

The grin that spread across Eve's lips was laced purely with lust. She kicked a foot onto the desk and lowered her hand to her crotch.

Jodi followed the motion, completely aware she was playing into Eve's game like a fool. If only she had real power in the presence of this sexy wench. If only.

Eve slowly circled her fingers over her clit. "Then you can watch."

Jodi couldn't look away as those fingers circled, flicked, and dipped inside wet walls. She lowered her hand to her own crotch and matched Eve. "Then so can you."

With her heart slamming against her chest, Eve flicked harder. She'd never been so brazen in her life, well, not outside her bedroom, and definitely only when Lexi was calling the shots. What the hell had come over her and where the fuck was all this courage coming from?

From Jodi's insinuation that she was an ice queen. No one had ever had the balls to say something like that about her, not when she was within a hundred feet of them, anyway. Just the sound of those words falling off her lips had made her horny.

Jodi moaned, working her fingers against her clit, alternating driving them inside herself. It was so fucking erotic—nasty and perverted in a controlled kind of way.

Fuck it!

Eve shoved off the desk and fell to her knees at Jodi's feet. She shoved her hand away and latched onto her. Jodi fisted her hair too tightly and Eve moaned, delightfully wet and humming against her clit. She slurped and sucked, unable to get enough of her scent, needing her insides pulsing strong around her tongue.

"Fuck yeah, Eve." Jodi drove her hips forward and then she was coming, using Eve's hair as reins, pulling her face harder and tighter against her pulsing pussy.

Eve lapped and drank, pressing against her clit, then back to sucking, until Jodi pulled her head back by a fistful of hair. She looked up under hooded lashes and licked her lips. "Yummy. Now me?"

Jodi yanked her off her feet and practically slammed her on the desk. She shoved Eve's legs wide and buried her face between her thighs. Eve cried out when her tongue curled around her swollen clit, praying no one had wandered too far down the deserted back half of the building. They were in for a surprise if they did.

That tongue lifted the base of her hood and Eve's hips rose with the action. Then Jodi latched on and Eve shoved against her face, grinding in deep, desperate circles.

"Get inside me, Jodi. Please fuck me!" Eve thrashed against the oak, out of her mind with the heat swarming down her limbs. She needed something solid filling her, and she now knew from experience that Jodi's fingers could more than do the trick.

Jodi loosed her suctioned hold and Eve's clit bobbed with need. "Where do you want me, Eve?"

Eve pulled her head forward, unsure exactly what she was asking, yet knowing the full meaning of the question. Could she, did she dare?

Jodi wasn't Lexi. Nor were they engaging in anonymous phone sex. "Anywhere. Everywhere. Do it, Jodi. Fucking hurry!"

Jodi coaxed her clit into a stiff peak with her tongue as Eve dropped her head back to the desk, her legs wide, her nipples straining against her bra so hard it was painful. Then Jodi was licking her again, slow, easy glides along her opening, up, up, over her clit, stabbing her tongue against her hood, and then drawing the bead into her mouth.

Eve couldn't take any more. Her orgasm was riding the waves of a hurricane, thrashing and pounding at her mind, at her core, at her pussy. Her walls clenched once and then Jodi was inside her, filling and fucking and driving.

"Yes!" Eve shoved her fingers into the strands of Jodi's hair and held tight.

Jodi probed at her ass once, twice, three times, pressing the tip of her finger at the entrance. Eve froze with anticipation, with blinding need. When Jodi pushed past the resistance, Eve whimpered. Slow and easy, she withdrew and entered, retracted and penetrated, over and over and fucking over again.

"Oh, yes, yes."

Jodi buried her fingers deep and then sucked at Eve's clit like it was her own personal pacifier.

Eve's orgasm shattered, washing over her in reckless bouts of hot heat. She screamed and clawed as wave after wave of liquid fire devoured her.

Jodi hummed and moaned, locking Eve's clit in her suctioned hold and then releasing the pressure to lap and drink.

Finally, the vigorous grips simmered and Eve drooped against the desk.

Jodi withdrew and ran light kisses along her leg and stomach. "You know, screams like that can give a girl a big head. I might not fit back through the door."

"I have a feeling I'm not the first girl to come screaming beneath that tongue. You should be past the macho strut and home-run trot." Eve wrestled to a sitting position and found Jodi smiling.

"And I have a feeling this isn't your first trip to this long-forgotten office."

Eve shrugged. Fact was, it wasn't. However, it was definitely the first time someone had made her bellow like a banshee. "A girl's gotta do what a girl's gotta do." She slid off the desk and pulled on her jeans and boots.

A green-eyed demon clawed at the surface and Jodi looked away to fight off the jealousy. She'd fucked more women than a black book could hold, and the thought of one woman laying her hands on Eve had her snarling like a raging bull. What the hell was wrong with her? She had no ties to Eve. At all. Well, except that long-distance private line, where she was tied in all the right places. But not here in the real world. Here, there were no strings attached. Eve was going to fly back to her life and she wasn't going to look back. Of that, Jodi was positive. Though it left a little hole in her, she was okay with it. She would live to see another day and another fuck. She knew what had been at stake before she took the chance to wait outside the studio in the pouring rain. Those facts wouldn't change today, tomorrow, or even when Eve boarded the flight to take her home. Eve wasn't hers. Not in flesh form, anyway.

Yet not two minutes ago, right now, and possibly for the rest of the week, Eve was hers. All fucking hers.

"Amelia is throwing me a stupid birthday party." The words were out of Jodi's mouth before she could trap them. Now she couldn't retract them. Amelia was going to kill her. She turned around to find Eve wearing a curious expression.

"Aww. How sweet." Eve's sarcastic laugher cut through the tension like a sharp knife.

"Yeah, whatever." She palmed Eve's hips and tugged her forward. "Be my date. Don't make me endure it alone. Please."

Eve's brow arched. "Hmm. Begging. I like that. What's the catch?"

"Well, if I know Amelia, there'll be party hats and streamers, trick candles and pink frosting, and lots of people I won't even know." Jodi kissed her chin. "Feel sorry for me and say you'll go."

"When?"

"Tonight."

"How old."

"A girl never tells." When Eve cocked her brow, Jodi hung her head. "Forty."

Eve laughed and Jodi kissed her, shutting off the sounds

immediately. "Mmmm." She pushed Jodi back. "Okay, fine. I'll do it. But on one condition."

Jodi envisioned Amelia with a devilish grin on her lips while she wrote her obituary. She was in so much trouble.

"Name it."

"You don't make me wear a party hat, and I get to scream around that tongue again tonight."

Jodi fanned her hands over Eve's narrow waist. "Damn, you drive a hard bargain. Deal."

"Good. Now go to work."

Jodi kissed her again, slicking her tongue against Eve's until she moaned, then she drew back and left the room.

Eve lingered behind, wondering what had possessed her to say yes to a lame birthday party. Maybe it was that pouty mouth or the serious eyes. Or maybe it was the more obvious—that she wanted more of those mind-blowing orgasms.

The flare of her nostrils when Eve admitted she'd christened this very room before. Maybe Eve was curious what could trigger such a reaction from a woman she was positive wouldn't think twice about their weeklong fling.

Eve still couldn't shake the feeling that Jodi felt familiar.

And she wondered why she didn't have a girlfriend.

Or how the hell she afforded that spectacular condo.

CHAPTER TWELVE

E ve had to laugh when Amelia opened the door wearing a party hat. Over her shoulder, she saw a "Lordy, Lordy, Jodi's Forty" banner draped above a mantle. Beyond the room, party horns whirred in high-pitched whistles.

"Oh, Eve, Khandi. I had no idea you were coming." Amelia stepped to the side to allow her and Khandi inside. "Please come in. What a surprise."

"Jodi invited us. Hope that's okay." Eve had a sneaky suspicion there was a reason why Amelia wore an unpleasant expression, but it was too late to turn back now. She looked around the room in hopes of finding Jodi. Truth was, she couldn't wait to run her tongue over that grooved tummy.

Balloons drifted across the ceiling in every hue of the rainbow and almost everyone wore matching party hats. Light music drifted from an adjoining room.

Eve gave Amelia the present she'd scurried to buy last minute. Okay, that was a lie. Out of anxiety, she'd dragged Khandi to the nearest shopping strip to buy Ozzy Osbourne's new release and couldn't resist buying the same for Jodi. Fact was, she didn't know anything about Jodi—what she liked or hated, her favorite music or her clothing size. If anything, every time Jodi skipped past the CD, she'd think of Eve and laugh at her peculiar choice of music. "Jodi's in the kitchen filling the punch bowl. Beware. She can be deadly with a vodka bottle."

Khandi grabbed Eve's wrist and tugged her forward. "Someone said booze. I'm there."

They wove their way through the throng and down a short hall to a dining room that was open to the kitchen. There she found Jodi over a large crystal bowl full of pink liquid, vodka bottle poised over the rim. Khandi stopped behind her and pointed to her ass, a wiggle on her brow.

Eve sent her a warning glare then cleared her throat. "I hear you're the spike queen."

Jodi turned around and Eve found herself falling into those clear green eyes. She almost took a step back. Tonight Jodi wore loose-fitting jeans and a plain peach T-shirt that slicked over her athletic curves, outlining deep ridges across her belly.

A smile formed on her mouth, making a promise Eve couldn't wait to take her up on. "That I am. I need everyone drunk before Amelia breaks out the trick candles and ice cream."

"Well, are you going to pour me a glass or do I have to pretend we're bobbing for apples?" Khandi blew the hair back from her brow with a huff, as if preparing for the dunk.

Thirty minutes later, Jodi had taken Eve on a private tour of the house and garden, stolen a kiss under a lighted gazebo, and introduced her to people she obviously wasn't that close with. Some had to remind her of their name, others she didn't even bother trying to recall. Amelia seemed to be the only true friend in her presence. It was obvious their friendship was deep-rooted.

Eve felt a bit on edge to be in Jodi's personal space, to be in such a precious moment. The atmosphere was so laid back Eve wondered if it was real. She'd been to birthday parties, but nothing that didn't involve catering, and definitely not anything so down-to-earth. There wasn't a fancy dinner room or elaborate décor. Only family and very dear friends would invest the tender care put into the hats and silly decorations.

A memory flashed through her mind—her own birthday parties. Her mother had spared no expense to ensure every one of her birthdays involved a yard full of smiling children with laughter filling the air. She suddenly missed those priceless moments, being innocent and carefree. An odd emotion slithered through her consciousness. She missed her mom, wanted to hug her tight and say thank you for the fun life she'd ensured her daughter would remember for life.

Though laughter and fun chatter filled these particular rooms, it was different somehow, almost staged. Could it be possible that Jodi didn't have close friends? Was Amelia her only true ally in this big bad world?

Was Eve any different? Wasn't Khandi the closest thing she could call a friend? How had she done that? Pushed everything else from her life but her career?

Khandi's whoop pulled her attention away. She followed the sound and grinned when she found her in the middle of the living room now transformed into a dance area. Her smile was bright as she jumped up and down to an old Cyndi Lauper tune. The woman could brighten a funeral, and Eve was suddenly proud to have her not only as an assistant, but also as a friend.

Khandi motioned for her to join. She declined with a shake of her head. She didn't have to answer to anyone here, but on this turf, she still considered herself the boss. No matter how sexy her date was, she wouldn't embarrass herself.

The song changed to "You Can Leave Your Hat On," and the dancers immediately started grinding playfully, others more serious as they danced for their partners. She found herself tapping, her body automatically catching rhythm with the beat. Another drink and she might be tempted to sway against Jodi's hard frame.

She glanced sideways at her. Jodi was intently watching the gaggle of dancers. Then she turned to look at Eve. A faint smile lifted the corner of her mouth and she took Eve's hand and pulled her out onto the terrace.

Before Eve could mention how beautiful the view was of the garden, Jodi turned her against the house and pinned her down with a kiss. Her breath snagged in her throat as a stab of desire whipped through her. Heat sparked down her spine and exploded between her thighs. God, this woman had a way of controlling her with nothing more than an innocent dominant action.

Eve wanted to push her away, wanted to tell her that the intimate kisses and stolen moments of passion meant nothing, that when it was time for her to leave this country, this city, she'd do just that—leave. There wouldn't be long-distance dating, or cybersex, or anything, for that matter. She'd been down that relationship road and had no desire to revisit it anytime soon. But for some reason, she felt Jodi already knew those things, that she expected Eve to walk away and not look back.

Jodi slicked her tongue inside her mouth and Eve forgot what she was thinking. Hell, it seemed she even forgot how to breathe when she was against that rock-hard body. For now, there was sex in her itinerary. Great sex, as a matter of fact. There was nothing stopping Eve from enjoying their time in Jodi's bed.

Jodi hummed against her mouth and kneaded her ass in the palm of her hands. Eve's body responded, slicking juices against her slit. She couldn't wait for the night to end so she could drop Khandi off, then dive into another night of earth-shattering sex.

When Jodi pulled back, Eve wanted to reach for another kiss, wanted to wrap her entire body around Jodi and never let loose. Of course, she didn't. She composed herself and straightened when the crowd inside clapped wildly. Khandi was more than likely the center of attention right now, doing only God knew what. It was probably best she didn't investigate.

Without thinking, she wrapped her hand around the back of Jodi's neck and pulled her back down. Just one more kiss. Just one.

An hour later, the dancers had spent their energy and everyone crowded into the dining room. Amelia emerged from the kitchen carrying a homemade cake with row upon row of stick candles. The room broke into the happy birthday song.

Amelia put the cake down in front of Jodi and her smile was so genuine it made Eve's heart ache. She suddenly felt lonely. She had Khandi, but not like this. She wouldn't jump in front of a speeding truck to save Eve's life. Maybe for a pair of Jimmy Choos, but never for Eve.

What Jodi had was precious, priceless, and irreplaceable. And the way Jodi was nudging Amelia and smiling, it was obvious she knew it too. Amelia loved her, was her protector even if Jodi thought those roles were reversed.

Eve sighed at the interaction. She thought about her own life, her job, and her family. Something was missing from the equation. Genuine friendship, reunions with family, and unbreakable bonds. She had none of that.

Were those things major factors in life? Did they play a pivotal role in a person's success, both in business and as a decent human being?

Why the hell did it matter? She was successful. She'd been greedy along the way, but it didn't change the outcome. She'd made a damn good life for herself, and her friends, or lack thereof, couldn't change that.

She tilted her cup of punch and drained the contents, dismissing the questions. The answers didn't matter.

The crowd clapped as Jodi blew out the candles.

What had she wished for? Fame, fortune, happiness, and health?

Eve had only one wish—to speed up time so she could slip naked beneath that glorious body and come around that tongue again. She only had this week, and she wanted to spend every spare minute of it coming with Jodi.

❖

Jodi stuffed her hands in her pocket as she walked beside Eve along the Embankment toward her apartment. She was happy Eve had come to the party. She'd made the entire night endurable and worthwhile. Especially knowing Amelia was going to chew her a new asshole first thing in the morning.

"You know, after all my years putting on a show for Fashion Week, I've never taken time to enjoy the beauty of this city?" Eve tucked her hand around Jodi's elbow and squeezed in closer.

Jodi flinched. The action made her feel like the escort whore she was. It was the only delicate connection she allowed those who paid her. She refused to hold a "date's" hand. The act was too personal, and there was nothing personal about their business arrangement.

Eve seemed unaware of the turmoil that gentle touch was stirring in her or the way her body stiffened. Unable to stand another second with Eve's hand woven around her arm possessively, Jodi plucked it away and wove their fingers together.

She looked down just in time to see a concerned expression pass over Eve's face, then flicker away as she continued to scour her surroundings.

Holding Eve's hand felt right, completely comfortable and fitting. Yet strangely wrong. Jodi concentrated on her last real date. Monica? Two years ago now? Had she held her hand? Had it felt this way? If it had, she couldn't remember. Come to think of it, she wasn't sure she could refer to their few months of meeting at restaurants, an opera, and two midnight strolls, then fucking, as dating.

The sex had been great. But nothing as connected as this. A connection that had started the day Eve dialed Lexi's number, reluctant and hesitant to see their first sex session through. From there, the bond had only grown until Jodi found herself expecting the calls, starving for Eve's helpless cries.

"So, Jodi, what do you do in your spare time?" She squeezed Jodi's hand.

Jodi thought about the answer. Or rather, the lie she was going to use as an answer. Sad fact was, she didn't have spare time. Most of her waking hours involved planning for a date, arranging a date, or being on a date. Even when she relaxed at home, the sex phone line snatched away much of her time. She almost chuckled. The person with whom she spent the bulk of her spare time was Eve, but she could hardly reveal that fact.

She shrugged. "I shop. I'm a sucker for a bargain."

"You shop? Seriously?"

Jodi nodded and prayed Eve wouldn't ask anything further. She didn't necessarily hate shopping, but it wasn't the top of her priority list. When she forced herself into a clothing store, she usually stocked up for the entire year with the new trends and styles. It was imperative that she stay as close to fashionable as she could when ushering a celebrity onto the red carpet, but that didn't mean she had to spend every waking moment obsessed with it.

"How much farther?"

"To where?"

"Your condo. Where you're going to fuck me again."

A whirlwind of fire traveled in ribbons down Jodi's limbs. She looked at Eve's determined face. She knew beyond a shadow of a doubt, she was addicted to her unknowing client, a woman she could never have.

Chapter Thirteen

Eve stepped into Jodi's condo, this time filled with need instead of anxiety and uncertainty. Her pussy tightened in agreement. She was ready—slick and hard and horny.

Jodi casually led the way to the living room where that beautiful expanse of windows showcased the brightly lit city of London far below.

She dropped onto the couch and studied Eve with a cool and aloof expression.

Eve felt a little unease. She walked to the window and looked out over the river to hide her discomfort at the silence. "We have sort of the same views. You see a beautiful river. I see a breathtaking park."

"You definitely don't have the same view as me."

Eve turned to her. She found Jodi slouched against the couch as if she didn't have a care in the world, elbow on the armrest, chin on thumb, and a dangerous mixture of desire and dominance swarming in her eyes.

"I see a beautiful and breathtaking woman standing far away from me right now, looking delicious enough to chew. And she's fully clothed."

Eve swallowed and thought about leaning back against the glass for support. She didn't want Jodi to see her weakness. Hell, she didn't want to feel her weakness. Jodi had a way of using her words to master that quality that even Eve didn't know she possessed. The hard ass was putty in Jodi's field of vision.

"Take off your clothes, Eve."

Eve cocked a brow. She would have laughed had there been any indication that Jodi was kidding, but her expression remained cold and direct. "Here?"

"Now."

A soft laugh escaped Eve's lips. Nervous, yet excited, she glanced over her shoulder at the lights reflected in the water below and at the buildings in the distance.

Did she dare make such a bold move? Was Jodi going to give her a choice? Did she want her to?

When she turned back around, Jodi was there, hovering over her like an avenging angel, her eyes dark and sure and screaming "fuck me." Startled, Eve backed away until the cool surface of the window halted her.

"Now, Eve. Take them off," Jodi whispered, then turned and fluidly sat on the curved-back chair beside them. She quickly regained the casual slouch that was her trademark.

Eve took in several breaths and reasoned with herself. Wasn't this what she wanted? To lose control? To have Jodi rip it from her? Wasn't that what she more or less paid Lexi to do? To dominate her? To strip away her shield of reserve? But this was different. She couldn't slam a phone down when she felt uncomfortable. Hell, as strong as Jodi's legs appeared, she'd be lucky to run three feet before Jodi caught, tackled, and hopefully fucked her hard.

Jodi still watched her, her eyes searching, and her entire body relaxed.

Eve had a feeling she was a natural at getting women to do as she pleased. Maybe that's why she was single. No woman could catch her or tame her. She was unreachable and liked it that way. The thought of another woman, many women, standing against this glass, with Jodi's carnal stare eating them alive, made a demon roar to life. She flinched with the emotion. She wasn't used to jealousy. It didn't sit well in the pit of her stomach. Yet the growly sensation put her at ease for some reason, made her feel human for once.

She lifted her chin. She wasn't there to tame anyone or catch someone she didn't want to snare. There was no time for games. She was there to get fucked. And God knew those eyes promised just that.

She widened her stance, softly placing her stiletto boot against the white marble tile, her heart thundering. It was that exact moment, with the sound of her heel clicking erotically against the porcelain, that she realized how bright the room was. From the couch, to the curtains, to those retro winged-back chairs, to the floors and walls. Bright. Tan, cream, off-white, to white. Everything was so damn bright. Save for three jade pillows tossed on the couch and the jet-black TV screen, the room screamed sterile, and don't-fucking-touch.

Everything was modern and immaculate. A row of round candles stair-stepped along the center of a white wood and glass coffee table. A tall white lamp stood alone in a corner. Had the bedroom been just as impeccable? Eve struggled to remember, not knowing why she should care. She shouldn't. She wouldn't.

She focused on Jodi and brazenly drew the blouse apart to expose her naked breasts. Her hands trembled as she let the material drop from her grasp.

"Beautiful," Jodi said lightly, her eyes rich with need. She leaned forward and lazily hung an arm over her crossed leg. "More."

With heat assaulting her pussy, Eve snagged open her jeans, kicked off her boots, and wiggled the denim down her legs, leaving the pink silk thong.

Jodi's gaze skimmed over her bare chest, down her stomach, and stopped at her underwear. Eve's nipples hardened under the mental caress. "Take them off."

She wanted to refuse. God knew, she really did, though no sane woman would, or could. She was standing in front of a wall-to-wall window before the whole fucking city of London, even if they couldn't see her. But those daring eyes told her Jodi would accept nothing less than Eve's obedience. She wanted nothing more than to be obedient for her.

She pushed the thin material down and kicked them away.

"Good girl." Jodi rose from the chair and patted the vacant seat. "Come. Sit."

Eve stepped quickly to the chair, thankful she wouldn't be on display any longer.

"On your knees. Facing the window."

Eve swallowed a gasp when she looked up into that stern face and realized Jodi wasn't playing. At all. Her expression remained emotionless, waiting. "Jodi, I—"

"Now, Eve." Jodi took a step closer, inspecting Eve's erect nipples. "Stop pretending you don't want to."

Eve couldn't move. Her mind was consumed with questions about how Jodi could know so much about her. How she could read her fantasies through her eyes.

Jodi ran the tip of her finger over a rock-hard nipple, then twirled the tender edge between her thumb and forefinger, making Eve's pussy sting. "I'm waiting."

Eve studied her for several seconds, her pussy aching and clenching. She waited for a playful smile, but Jodi stood stock-still. Something in her demeanor told Eve to move, to obey Jodi's commands to the letter; that in doing so, she would reap every ounce of reward.

Hesitantly, Eve turned to face the chair. She knelt on the padding and gripped the curved back.

Her pussy clenched tight when Jodi came to stand behind her. "I think I like you this way. Open, exposed, and wet."

A strangled cry flew past her lips when Jodi dragged a single digit along her slit, then pushed her hood up, exposing her swollen tissue. She jerked into a bow and opened farther. Once again, she was on exhibition. This time in a most vulnerable position. This time not caring. The moment was too intense to give a shit about anything other than those skilled hands working her pussy like an artist.

"I could close the curtain, but this is too erotic. Your body against the expanse of such a beautiful night sky." Jodi shoved her hood higher and Eve hissed and spasmed.

Eve watched their reflection, how Jodi observed her own actions. Jodi drawing in the sight of Eve had her pussy clamping tight. And then Jodi closed her eyes as if savoring the moment. Eve could almost feel the entire room change moods.

Jodi let her eyes flutter shut with Eve's erotic whimpers. She stroked her clit, trapped the hardening tissue between two fingers, massaging and pinching, then flicking and circling, pulling incoherent sounds from Eve's throat.

If Eve only knew how nervous and unsure she was, how confused and in utter disbelief at her luck to have Eve here, naked and available for her taking, she'd turn around right now and race from this apartment and never look back.

Right now, Jodi was a disaster with Eve's flesh on her fingertips. She needed to get her head clear, needed to take a deep breath and swallow back indecision. From the second Eve had appeared in the doorway of Amelia's kitchen, a strange turmoil had taken hold of her mind, and the possibility of living a normal life, with a steady girlfriend, without "dates" and little black books, consumed her thoughts. She wanted a dog, maybe even a cat. She wanted to cook dinner and cuddle in bed to watch a late-night reality show.

Could she break routine? Could she alter her chosen path? Walk the straight and narrow with all the average, hardworking people? Like Amelia? Like Eve? Like the women at her party she barely knew? Was it hopeless to think she could live among them? Had she coveted this ride for too long? Could she jump ship this late in the game?

Eve bucked when Jodi scissored her fingers around her clit. Jodi opened her eyes to look up the expanse of Eve's spine, at the tattoo shaded in green-black, the dragon's eyes red and defensive and careening over her shoulder blade.

Then she caught Eve examining her in the glass. Her lips were parted, curiosity in her eyes. God only knew what Eve had read in her expression.

She draped herself over Eve and followed the tail and body of the artwork with her tongue, holding the misty reflection looking back at her. "You like watching yourself come, Eve?" She teased Eve's opening then pressed her index and middle finger inside.

Eve moaned. Sweet music. Jodi struggled not to close her eyes again.

It seemed Eve was struggling with the same thing. Her eyes fluttered. "I like watching you fuck me." Eve hissed through clenched teeth and lost control. She closed her eyes.

Jodi withdrew and with practiced skill forked two fingers to open Eve's slick lips, then lifted the hood of her clit again with her middle finger, exposing the sensitive area beneath.

Eve bucked. "Jesus, Jodi."

Jodi lifted away from Eve and memorized the delicate indentation trailing down to her rounded ass, how smooth and taut and tan her skin was, down to her own fingers stimulating pleasure between Eve's spread thighs.

Perfection. She was absolute perfection.

Right now, Jodi had perfection on her fingertips. She wanted to taste her, tongue-fuck her, drive inside her.

Desperate for Eve's flesh against her face, Jodi moved her hand

and knelt. She pushed open Eve's ass cheeks to expose her anus and her weeping pussy, then ran her tongue along her slit, tasting her arousal and inhaling her desire.

Eve cried out and a rumble of possession cracked from Jodi's soul. She licked faster, sucking and kissing her clit, lapping her juices in feverish swipes of her tongue, hungry and desperate for more.

Addicted. She was fucking addicted to everything about Eve. Her odor, her unbridled cries, her bossiness outside this room, her complete submission inside it. She wanted to fall on her flesh, wanted Eve thrashing against her, around her, in her.

"Get inside me, Jodi. Dear God, fuck me!"

Jodi inserted a single finger inside her, teasing her G-spot before trailing a wet path to the ringed muscle of her anus. She pressed once and Eve whimpered. Jodi flicked her clit with the tip of her tongue, then pushed her finger inside.

"Fuck, Jodi! I'm coming!" Eve loosed a raw scream and bucked.

Jodi wrapped her free hand around her waist and drove her mouth around Eve's clit, sucking and pulling, all while Eve surged backward against her face. Her pussy and ass pulsed with strong contractions as Jodi continued drinking from her, tasting her, starved for more.

Eve's body rocked and convulsed, her orgasm intense and clenching. Her arms folded and she bent completely over the bar of the chair, and then her knees gave way.

She had the sensation of falling and then she was secure in Jodi's arms, cradled against her hard chest like a victim, like some damn girl. Light-headed, she looked up into Jodi's smiling face.

"You should remember to breathe when you're coming." Jodi kissed her forehead, cheek, then the hollow of her throat. "But you sure know how to give a girl a big head."

"Don't flatter yourself, stud." Eve pushed out of her grasp and sat up, taking in her surroundings and the fact that she was now on the floor. Her head swam for a brief second then cleared. "Sex and lack of food. Does it every time."

"I tried to tell you those breakfast bars would be the death of you."

Eve slowly turned to look at her, Lexi's mockery of her eating habits ringing loud in her head.

Jodi looked stunned for a second, then quickly recovered by pulling Eve against her body and biting the skin at the crook of her neck and shoulders. "Figuratively speaking, that is. You've been eating them like candy around the studio."

Eve sighed. Her body hummed and tingled, and she wanted to do it again. Right now. God, she'd never felt anything so fucking incredible in her entire life. Leaving this one behind was going to be harder than she thought. Not hard enough, of course, but she was sure her dreams and memories were going to scorch her for a long while.

She inhaled to clear the fuzz from her mind, then rose and started across the cold marble floor. With a single glance over her shoulder, Eve stalled at the threshold to the master bedroom. "When you're done talking to yourself about health and nutrition, I'll be waiting. Wet. And ready for you. Again."

Jodi growled in heated lust when Eve disappeared into the room. She considered staying where she was to see if Eve would come back for her, to see how long it would take Eve to come back for her, then she thought better of it and shoved off the floor.

She slid to a halt at the door when she found Eve perched in the middle of her king-sized bed, backed against the iron bars, hands looped around two spindles, knees bent, and legs parted enough to glimpse sweet pink flesh.

A moan started in the pit of her stomach, then flew past her lips as a helpless mating whimper. She stalked to the bed.

Eve smiled, a devilish crook to her lips. "Stop!"

Jodi did, though she didn't know how. Her mind was already on the bed, pinning Eve to the mattress, bucking inside her.

"See that black tie?" Eve nodded toward the closet.

Jodi gave a single incline of her head, unable to turn away from the feast laid out before her.

"Bring it to me."

Their roles obviously reversed, not that she cared, Jodi darted for the tie looped over the hat rack on the back of her closet door and ripped the fabric from the hook. When she turned back, Eve was on her knees at the foot of the bed.

Eve patted the edge. "Come. Sit."

Jodi obediently obliged, albeit with a hint of reluctance.

"Scoot back to the headboard."

With a shove, Jodi slid backward across the mattress until she was wedged against the cold steel.

Eve crawled up the bed and straddled her thighs. She ground her pussy down hard and grabbed Jodi's hands as they wove around her delicate thighs. "Not so fast, tiger. A girl needs to catch her breath, you know?"

With speed Jodi never knew something so petite could possess, Eve shoved her hands against the iron. Her face void of any emotion, she wound the tie around Jodi's wrists, twice, and then knotted it around a bar.

Eve sat back on her heels and eyed her captive. Sexy couldn't touch the description of Jodi. Her hair was perfectly tousled, her long legs stretched out, and that tight tummy waiting for Eve's lips. And her eyes were packed with a desire so deep that the sight scared Eve. She'd never seen passion so thick.

She lowered herself across Jodi's body and sucked her lower lip between her teeth.

When Jodi groaned, she traced her upper lip, corner to corner, and then slicked her tongue inside. Heat gathered in her stomach, and she palmed Jodi's face to hold herself in check, to keep from whimpering like a lovesick fool at the intensity engulfing her.

She could very well become addicted to this kind of sex, with this particular woman. Who could blame her? Jodi was a walking advertisement for sex. And here Eve was, the center of her attention, her focal point, unable to get enough, knowing full well she'd never forget a second of this night, of this week.

She pulled back and Jodi attempted to follow. The tie halted her advances, and she fell back against the bars with a gruff growl.

Eve slid down her body, unbuttoning her shirt as she lowered herself, stopping only to assault those cut muscles lining her stomach, licking and nipping, needing to bite and chew until she felt satisfied and full. Then she slipped between Jodi's thighs and tugged the rivet of her jeans open with her teeth.

Jodi could barely breathe, yet could barely not, and she couldn't look away.

She'd never wanted anyone so ferociously in her life. The need was like a constant ache in her gut, curling and tightening into pain. She'd never felt anything like it.

Eve tugged Jodi's jeans down and studied her white mid-thigh briefs with a twinkle in her eye.

This was a mistake. All of it. Every minute of their time together was only making her miserable, making her think about things that just couldn't be. Eve wasn't available. Neither was Jodi. Yet the facts couldn't stop the runaway images assaulting her thoughts.

She wasn't normal. She was an escort. A whore to the rich with nothing to offer Eve, nothing but a used-up body that had made love to hundreds of women. No one in their right mind would want her.

Eve tugged her underwear down and off then thumbed her lips apart. Jodi snapped her thoughts away and tugged at her bindings in desperation to reach for Eve, to slip her fingers into those long, dark strands, to pull her face harder against her crotch.

With the pressure of Eve's tongue along her clit, lifting her hood over the sensitive flesh beneath, Jodi rose off the mattress and slammed her head into the bars. "Ah, fuck!"

Eve drew the flesh into her mouth and flicked her tongue against the tip.

Jodi pumped toward that pleasing mouth, her orgasm scrambling so fast to the razor-sharp edge that it blinded her with cruel intensity. She fought back the urge to release, desperate for control, not to come so damn fast. Eve sucked harder, her hungry moans vibrating against Jodi's pussy. Lights flashed behind her closed lids and then her body dissolved into liquid convulsions.

Visions of Eve draped over the chair—the depth and darkness of the night sky stretching beyond the window, her reflection staring back at Jodi packed full of desire—flashed through her mind as her orgasm ripped through her body. She hissed and cussed, tugged, pumped, and shattered, and then she went limp against the mattress and bars.

She lay still, eyes screwed tight as her body tingled. She struggled to remember the last time she'd allowed a woman to make love to her, to touch her, the way Eve had. The answer wasn't readily available. She'd slept with hundreds. Yet only allowed a rare few women to reciprocate. None of whom were paying.

Stone-hearted. That's what Amelia called her. Was that what

she was? Stony, cold, withdrawn? Or realistically holding tight to the only thing that kept her sane, seeing it as the job that it was? Nothing personal.

When Eve shifted between her thighs, Jodi cracked her lids open. Her lips were glossy from Jodi's arousal, her come, her release, and then she licked them, a slow savoring of her tongue from one corner of her upper lip to the other.

Jodi jerked at her binding, wanting Eve's flesh on her face, in her mouth, bucking beneath her body so badly she almost begged. Almost.

"Untie me."

Eve only smiled and sat back. She fanned her legs open, exposing pink flesh. "You see, Jodi, I'm not very savvy to these domination games—role playing, control ripping, whatever the hell it's called, but I do know one thing; there's a safe word involved, and you didn't give me one before you so willingly allowed me to tie you up." She licked her middle finger, then eased her hand between her legs.

Jodi couldn't have dragged her gaze away if the devil himself appeared and offered her a cool spot in hell. She yanked against the bars with an animalistic snarl. "Eve, don't."

"Isn't it so much more exciting to look when you can't touch?" Eve drove two fingers inside herself. She threw her head back and arched into her hand.

Desperation whipped down Jodi's limbs. To gain release. To be the one drilling her fingers inside Eve, fucking her. She twisted her wrists, only managing to tighten the knot.

Eve's stomach muscles bunched as she rocked against her hand, her fingers slick with her own juices. "What do I look like, Jodi? Right now, fucking myself?" She pulled her fingers out, then she pushed them back inside, once again arching as her pussy swallowed their length.

Something sharp snapped inside Jodi. She wrenched her arms forward and hissed in pain. "Eve, dammit, untie me!"

"Tell me."

Jodi relaxed her arms and watched those fingers glide so deep. "Sexy, erotic." She wriggled her wrists, finally loosening the pressure. "I'm going to fuck you, Eve. So fucking hard."

Eve withdrew and opened her lips to expose her swollen clit. She dragged her finger up the base, over the hood, unsheathing the delicate tissue beneath. Then she flicked and cried out. "Do I look like a two-bit slut?"

Jodi froze, breath hanging in her throat like thick fog. Her heart slammed against her chest. She'd said those words to Eve. Lexi had said them.

Without waiting for an answer, Eve fell back against the mattress, her middle finger flicking faster, her hips rocking and pumping. Her dark nipples stood erect, tight and needy. "I'm, ah, shit. Jodi, I'm coming!"

Her body thrashed, severing Jodi's sanity.

She ripped at the bindings in a hungry, desperate rage. The material gave way and she bucked off the bars just as Eve's hips rose from the mattress.

Jodi fell over her and entered her in one swift, hurried thrust.

Eve's pussy clenched hard around her. She screamed, arms and nails digging down Jodi's spine, her legs and ankles locking around her body.

Jolt after jolt, Jodi fucked her, her head buried in the crook of Eve's neck, her back muscles bunching as she arched and pumped deep inside her.

Those sweet cries flowed into the room, into her mind, ripping into her soul.

Jodi closed her eyes tightly, once again assaulted by those desperate cries.

CHAPTER FOURTEEN

Jodi stepped around a gentleman checking his mail in the lobby of her condo and spotted Amelia on the sidewalk. Even through the double-pane glass, Jodi could see the tension in her folded arms and in her stiff-straight posture. Her lips were thin and tight with the scowl that had seemed to be an on-again-off-again feature for the past days.

She thought about turning around and going right back up to her apartment, but she'd weathered fiercer storms than Amelia.

Amelia spotted her and her entire faced transformed, eyes narrowing into blue chips of icy anger. Okay, so maybe she hadn't weathered anything more ferocious.

Jodi drew in a breath, pushed through the doors, slowly stepped out onto the sidewalk, and hesitantly approached her, preparing for the outburst Amelia could have easily let loose last night when she opened the door to find her boss on the stoop. Jodi should have told her, should have warned her that she'd asked Eve to the party, but she just couldn't bring herself to say the words for fear that Amelia would rain on her parade, would remind her what an idiot she was being.

"Have you lost your damn mind, Jodi?"

Jodi held up her hands defensively. "Can we at least move away from my neighbors before you scream at me?" She turned and started toward the Westminster Bridge, anxious to begin the day, to see Eve again.

She'd left early, like a whirlwind of hair and flesh, rushing into each item of clothing, bouncing on one leg to get her jeans on, barely stopping long enough to wave good-bye to Jodi. The fast-paced action hadn't made Jodi feel like it was a mad dash to exit her apartment, to get away. It was part of Eve's life—always in a hurry, always rushed.

Amelia fell in beside Jodi, her tennis shoes hard against the pavement as each stomp punctuated her words. "Would it have been too much trouble for my best friend to warn me that my hopefully new boss was going to show up on my doorstep? Are you trying to drive me crazy, not to mention fucking with my career?"

"How the hell could that ruin your career?" Jodi moved around a slower couple, wishing she'd showered much faster this morning. She could do without this particular argument after the glorious night she'd spent with Eve, making love to her, and being made love to.

"If she finds out about you, I can kiss everything good-bye. How many times do I have to repeat myself? I've worked my ass off to get in with a company like hers, Jodi, and you're going to fuck it up, all for a fuck."

Jodi stopped to face Amelia. No use taking another step until Amelia had gotten it all out. She struggled to find the right words to calm her down. Fact was, there weren't any. Another fact: Eve was a very satisfied woman right now, details she wouldn't share with Amelia.

Her insides cramped at the mere thought of her night with Eve, and she had to focus on early-morning joggers to shove the erotic images from her mind.

"Calm down, Mel. She's not going to find out. Everything is under control. Trust me. I promise."

Amelia's jaw tightened. "I see your mouth moving, but all I hear is blah blah blah."

Jodi grinned and leaned close. "Then wipe John's come out of your ear so you can hear me better."

Amelia's eyes danced with anger and then she burst out laughing at the reference to one of her former phone clients—a man who had a fetish for coming in a woman's ear, especially Amelia's.

"You're a dog. You know that?"

"Woof. But you love me."

Amelia's eyes softened. "Seriously, Jodi. You're headed for trouble, and you're going to drag me right down with you." Amelia closed her hand around Jodi's. "You need to end this, whatever it is, before someone gets hurt. Me, first and foremost, since I'm the one person who'll put up with your shit." She grinned playfully, though it never touched her eyes. "Eve second. I'm pretty sure she'd be a very upset woman to find out who you are and what you do for a living. She might be okay with the sex operator part, but not so much to find out you fuck for a fee."

Jodi cringed at her words, somehow hearing them for what they really were. Fucking for a fee. That's what she did, who she was.

Amelia gave her hand a squeeze. "I'm sorry. That was harsh."

Jodi returned the squeeze. Amelia was right. But her moments with Eve felt so right, so real. She wanted this time, this freedom. All the innocence it brought. She deserved it. "She's not going to find out, Amelia. Fashion week is almost over. It ends there."

"It begins there, Jodi. It began the minute you took her home." She drew in a breath and glanced down the sidewalk. "Hell, probably the minute I asked you to help me. I'm such an idiot."

"What's that supposed to mean?" Jodi couldn't help but feel a stab of pain.

"Your face, Jodi, all over the tabloids. She's going to find out, whether you like it or not. Whether I like it or not. It's just a matter of time." Panic tripped across her expression. "It's my fault. I'm doomed."

Jodi not only heard her unraveling, she saw it as well. She hated herself for making Amelia worry, all for her own self-satisfaction. "You're not doomed. And you make it sound like my face is the only focal point of every cover. That couldn't be further from the truth."

Amelia looked away, her focus on nothing in particular. "It's close enough, Jodi. Don't try to bullshit me. Just last week you were on the red carpet with Carlotta. Very visible."

"That was last week. Already history. And don't you think my cover would have already been blown if Eve bored herself with London gossip?"

Amelia nodded. "True, I suppose…" She studied Jodi with an uncertain expression. "You're smitten with her, aren't you?"

Jodi chuckled. "Intrigued, maybe. I've never been *smitten* a day in my life."

The steady look on Amelia's face proved she didn't believe Jodi. "Intrigued how?"

Jodi thought for a moment, not sure she knew the answer, or if there was an answer. "What would a woman like her, who has it all, who could have anyone, anytime, any day, want in a sex operator, in nothing more than a phone voice?"

She let the remaining statement rest in her mind. What did Eve want in Lexi? Why Lexi? Why Jodi?

"Because she has to and because she can. Nothing more, nothing less. You've seen firsthand the way she lives her life, always rushing, people drilling her every minute of every day, jostling and tugging for her attention." Amelia pulled Jodi forward and started walking. "I completely understand her. It's probably the only thing she has that's close to a relationship. Hell, if I walked in her shoes, I'd do the same. It's the perfect commitment."

Jodi pondered her words. Was that truly the reason? Because she had no other choice if she wanted her sexual thirst quenched? Was their phone connection all she was privy to? All she had time for?

"But that's not the question, is it?"

Jodi narrowed her eyes. "What is the question?"

"You want to know why she keeps coming back to Lexi."

Jodi looked away, confused by those sympathetic eyes, hating that Amelia could read her so easily.

What was it that Jodi possessed that Eve couldn't get enough of, that she craved? More than anything else, she wanted answers to that question. Almost as much as she wanted to know how Eve could trigger deep-rooted emotions with a whimper. "Yes."

Amelia blew out a long, low whistle. "I take it back. Eve's not going to get hurt, and neither am I." She pulled Jodi close to her. "You are."

❖

Eve studied her feet as the manicurist applied a dark shade of maroon while Khandi chattered nonstop from the chair beside her, thumbing through yet another magazine. Her new obsession was starting to worry Eve. Khandi barely read her to-do lists around the office, let alone articles in a foreign magazine, and definitely not every sentence.

The day wasn't over just yet. She still had to contend with the night—the final walk-through, with the models wearing their assigned gowns, suits, and outfits. After that, everyone would hopefully enjoy a few drinks and relaxation before a good night's sleep, and then all hell would break loose as soon as they stepped foot inside the theater with the morning light, the grand finale.

She was tired, anxious, and nervous about tomorrow. Everything was running smoothly, just as predicted. Her mind ached like a dull throb she could feel forming in the back of her skull, right at the base of her neck. She'd been unusually fidgety throughout the day, especially when Jodi and Amelia had arrived. Something was different about the air around them, as if they were both off-kilter, void of their normal fun laughter.

It'd left her feeling uneasy and awkward.

She'd been tempted to inquire about their lack of chatter, but that would have meant she had to approach Jodi, something she didn't trust herself to do. Images had spilled through her mind all day, robbing her of the clear conscious she needed to see that her fashion show was perfect.

Damn, she was doing it again—thinking about Jodi, seeing every inch of her with such clarity. It was disturbing, how she couldn't wrestle Jodi away mentally—those hands, that mouth, those dominating traits. That's all it was. After a few more hours of staring models down, she was going to do it all over again. She was going to come, hard, with Jodi's name erupting from her mouth, and tomorrow she'd witness a well-run fashion show, then do it all over again for the last time.

She was seriously going to miss those artistic hands, all the moans and screams they'd managed to rip from her body, from the very core of her soul.

With a start and afraid she'd done something ridiculous, like moan out loud, Eve turned to Khandi. "Do you go anywhere without those damn tabloids anymore? What's up with you and foreign gossip lately?" Happy that she'd said all those words without a quiver to her voice, she stretched back in the chair, enjoying the relaxing minutes, her pamper time before fuck time—less than twenty-four hours before crunch time.

"I told you, I'm keeping my eye on things for you."

"Really? Like for sketches from my competitors?"

"No." Khandi threw a bored glance in her direction.

"Like somebody poaching my new designs?"

"No, smart-ass. And who cares about fashion with all these hotties appearing on the front pages?" Khandi flipped to another page. "You should take a peek."

"Ah, here we go again with hotties in magazines." Eve studied her more carefully. She wore a bright do-rag on her head today that matched the T-shirt with a peace symbol dominating the front.

"Speaking of hotties, you never told me about you and Jodi." She wiggled her brow.

When Eve closed her eyes, Khandi huffed. "Fine. You don't have to tell me about Jodi. I'll just read about her in the tabloids."

Eve snickered. "Wow, she's that important that she gets the spotlight of the front cover? Maybe I should reconsider reading every article." She angled her head. "Hmm. There, I've thought about it. I'll pass."

"Your loss."

"I'll live."

"We'll see." Khandi tossed the magazines in the trash can by her chair.

Eve relaxed as the beautician rubbed oil onto her feet and massaged up her calves.

Stronger hands were going to take the same route later tonight. They were going to travel beyond the bend of her knee, past her quivering inner thighs, and slide sweetly into her dripping depths.

Her insides clenched.

❖

Eve stood at the end of the temporary catwalk in the studio, watching the models sashay through the test walk, stalling, posing, and then turning to reverse their paths back along the runway. Her newest creations, in all their glorious sleekness, were hours away from the real fashion show, from the genuine catwalk a few blocks away at the theater. This was the last opportunity she'd have to change her mind, or change a model to another gown, or vice versa. This walk-through meant everything. Any and every flaw should and must be caught.

The area was packed; shrill voices climbed over one another as each model made her way through the entrance. Francesca stood on the edge of the platform, pincushion around her wrist, halting a model here and there for an adjustment. The hair and makeup artists scurried after their chosen models, checking curls and hairpins or lipstick and mascara.

Eve didn't have to see Jodi to know she was present. But the fact that she'd witnessed her and Amelia squeezing through the crowd was a bonus. It gave Eve time to rein in her control and move to the opposite side of the catwalk to be farther away from her. She still didn't trust herself to be too close.

Even the ice queen had her limits. Seemed Jodi was Eve's breaking point, where all business seemed to come unraveled, leaving her frazzled and confused, desperate to get back on track.

Though she was overwhelmed and rushed, her ego was bursting. Every item of clothing—from the raw and rare fabric, to the modern pieces of jewelry—was fabulous. She was thrilled with her choices and positive the show would be a hit.

Finally, the last model turned at the end of the runway and stepped off the platform. They all scurried after Francesca to the fitting room, all crews in close attendance.

Eve fell into an empty chair with a sigh, her body a tight bundle of nerves. Or was it tight with anticipation of her night with Jodi? She couldn't tell anymore.

Khandi dropped into the chair beside her. "Looks like another hit, boss."

Eve nodded and looked around. Jodi and Amelia were tucked into the same corner they had been all night, watching the action with skeptical eyes. She was positive Amelia studied everything for business reasons—wrapping her head around the fast-paced life she might possibly be stepping into. Or praying she could step into if everything went to plan for a permanent contract. As for Jodi, she studied Eve a little too often. The needy expression on her face made Eve weak.

"Come, you two. Relax." Eve motioned to them. "Share your thoughts on the dress rehearsal."

They made their way across the room and took the chairs closest to Eve, Jodi farther away. Eve smiled. Jodi looked so out of place. Even now, with the calm of the first wave of the storm past them. Was Eve the reason for her discomfort? She liked that idea.

"I know you two aren't new to this kind of backstage mayhem, but what did you think about Eve's chaotic world?" Khandi asked.

"To be honest, I loved the controlled aspect." Amelia looked over the erected runway. "It was calming to see how well you had your shit together. How everyone had everything under control, even if it didn't appear that way. I especially liked envisioning my props at the end."

Eve liked her response. It was nice to see that someone had noticed the fact that she ran a tight ship, leaving little room for mistakes, though mistakes were bound to happen whether she liked it or not. She hired only the best, expected nothing less out of all of them. Her gut told her Amelia would fit in perfectly with her fashion family. Tomorrow would prove all—how Amelia handled herself under pressure, how fast she got her props onto the set for Eve's spot, then off again for the next in line.

"As well you should. They're beautiful. And I take pride in my employees." Eve glanced at Khandi. "Well, some of them."

Khandi huffed playfully. "Keep it up, witch, and I'll hide your damn cell phone."

Jodi perked at the mention of a cell phone.

"Hmmm. I wonder if you'd miss your London tabloids as much as I'd miss my phone." Eve smirked as Khandi looked Jodi's way for a brief second, then flicked back to Eve.

Jodi swallowed hard. Did Khandi know? If so, why hadn't she busted Jodi long before now? Was it her overworked imagination playing tricks again?

"I'd miss them long enough to walk to the corner vendor to purchase more. Brand-new ones. Such juicy information you can find in every one of them." Once again, Khandi studied Jodi.

Amelia shifted uneasily in her chair, but Jodi refused to look away.

"My money's on Roger. I bet he'd have a new phone in my grasp before you could get to the sidewalk." Eve turned to Jodi and Amelia. "You both live here. Is there really that much interesting in these tabloids she's obsessed with?"

Jodi shrugged. "I don't read the crap." She gave Khandi a hard stare, just in case she was playing some kind of mind game. "Most of it is bullshit. Can't believe what you read in the papers."

A smile bounced off Khandi's lips. "I agree. But some things are definitely true. You just have to ask the right people." She leaned back in her chair and laid her clipboard on her lap. A magazine slid to the edge and she caught it. Jodi glimpsed the edge of a red carpet; her stomach lurched violently in the certain knowledge more of the page would show her face standing to the side waiting for Carlotta to pose for the paparazzi. "Do you happen to know Carlotta Tate? She's, like, a major theater icon around here, right?"

Jodi's jaw tightened and her blood pressure spiked. What the hell was Khandi up to? Why hadn't she blown Jodi's cover long before now?

"Oh, brother. Now we've got her started." Eve rose and motioned for Jodi and Amelia to follow. "We have reservations for drinks across the street in thirty. Will you both join us?"

Jodi jumped from her chair, anxious to end the conversation.

Eve started walking without waiting for the rest of them. "Khandi, round up everyone else who wants to come. Tell them drinks are on me."

"Aye, aye, sir."

Jodi took in a breath of fresh air as they pushed out onto the sidewalk, thankful for the first time that it wasn't raining as the weatherman had predicted. Her heart was still catapulting.

Amelia fell back and grabbed Jodi's arm. "What the fuck was that all about?"

Jodi rubbed her chin. "I don't know, Amelia. I'm so sorry."

Amelia gave her arm a gentle squeeze. "Don't be. It's really not your fault. Well, not all of it." She glanced toward Eve. "We had no way of knowing my boss and your client would be one and the same."

"I know. But that doesn't make me feel any better right now." They waited for a car to pass before following Eve across the street. Eve slipped inside the bar with a backward glance.

Amelia jerked Jodi to a stop. "I'm not sure you have a choice. You might have to tell her before that little twat back there spills the beans. It'll be worse coming from someone else."

Jodi's gut churned as her mind filled dangerously fast with the many different scenarios of the outcome. "Which part? That I fuck for a fee, as you put it so succinctly? Or that I make her come a few nights a week through her cell phone?"

Amelia studied her for several seconds. "Shit. Neither. Both. I don't fucking know. It's too much drama. I can't think." She glanced toward the bar. Her eyes narrowed. "Okay, if the twat hasn't said anything yet, then she's hesitating for a reason. Right? All you have to do is keep Eve busy. You can do that. Right?"

Jodi draped her arm around Amelia's shoulder. "Come on, frazzle brain. Let's go get you a drink."

"Yeah, like alcohol will make it all go away." Amelia stalled outside the bar door. "Whatever happens, just remember I love you. Okay?"

"I love you too. But you're still going to toss my ass in the river if all hell breaks loose, correct?"

"Correct."

With a smile, Jodi led her inside.

Chapter Fifteen

The reserved bar was crowded and loud, but relaxed and comfy as everyone laughed, letting the stress of the day dissolve. Eve always enjoyed this particular night—the night before the showdown—when everyone was at their peaked high with anxieties overloaded. Yet mixed in the chaos was tranquility and calmness, like the eye of the hurricane.

The back side of the storm would come bright and early tomorrow, and together, they would all rush like wild tigers for the kill.

Eve sipped her wine and found Jodi sitting with Amelia. They were talking quietly to each other. She was now positive something was amiss between the two of them, though what, she couldn't put a finger on.

She suddenly thought of Lexi. Twice in the past few days she'd attempted to call her, only to get a recorded message saying she was unavailable right now. That was unlike her. Eve made a mental note to call her later. Before she left this building, or maybe after she fucked Jodi.

Her insides heated with the thought and then an immediate dread washed over her. Tonight, then tomorrow night, and her time with Jodi would come to an end.

She wasn't sure how she felt about that. A little sad maybe?

Low murmurs filled the room and Eve turned to find Zara weaving through the crowd, her height making her almost a head taller than most of the gathering. Late, as usual. She'd always needed a grand entrance to boost her ego, as if everyone in the room had been waiting with bated breath for her entrance alone, as if she were one of the models, or even a damn designer. Her following stayed close to her, all with their heads high, knowing they were walking behind royalty. She was, of course, but it irked Eve that everyone treated her as such.

Eve made her way to the bar for a refill, not wanting to appear too eager to greet Zara. She leaned against the counter, ordered a Crown and Coke, then felt body heat close to her. Familiar body heat. With a breath hanging in her throat, she turned to find Jodi standing beside her.

Her libido instantly coiled tight, automatically slicking juices between her thighs.

"How much longer do I have to watch you prance around this room before I can take you home to fuck you?" Jodi whispered.

Eve's breath fluttered in her throat like a trapped bird. Jesus, what was this woman doing to her? "There's a bathroom right around the corner." She took a sip of her drink. "We don't have to wait at all."

A smile flicked across Jodi's lips. "That's very tempting. But the way I want to make you scream tonight, I think privacy might be in order."

Eve looked away, positive she'd moaned out loud. Her pussy was scalding hot, and her insides felt like someone had run her through a meat grinder.

"With promises like that, how could a girl refuse?" Eve pushed away from the counter. "Give me ten minutes and I'm taking you up on that offer."

Eve made her way quickly to Zara, placing her sweetest smile in place. She kissed her cheek and sat across from her.

Before Eve could make pleasant conversation, Zara leaned across the table. "You must really be doing well for yourself, my dear. She doesn't come cheap." Zara looked toward the bar and pursed her lips with vicious amusement.

Eve was terrified to look, but more afraid not to. She slowly turned her attention on Jodi, exactly where Zara was staring. A lump swelled in her throat.

All the little pieces of the puzzle slammed into place, forming a picture-perfect image before her.

The older woman at the restaurant, the billboard clothing, the way she worked those hands like a master, that immaculate condo Eve wasn't sure even she could afford, and the way she wouldn't answer Eve's questions about her day job.

A hooker. She'd been sleeping with a fucking hooker.

Jodi was still perched on a stool, and her brow cocked at Eve's immobile stare. Then something flickered in her eyes. Regret? Shame? Remorse? Fear?

Eve took in a shallow breath, refusing to turn a startled expression back on Zara, damned if she'd let her see her squirm. Warning bells sounded in her head as she forced a grin in place and turned to face Zara.

Eve put her mouth against her ear and whispered, "Sweetie, you must be getting rusty in your old age. She does me for free."

Eve begged the heavens above that her words wouldn't change the outcome of the fashion show, knowing full well it would if she didn't take recovery action immediately. Zara was an immature brat who wouldn't hesitate to fuck up Eve's event by pulling her money out of every sale.

She pushed away from the table with only a quick glance at Zara's shocked gasp. One foot in front of the other, she strode across the room.

❖

Jodi couldn't move as Eve barreled toward her, hating herself for not taking those quiet two minutes to take Eve aside and tell her the truth. She'd missed her opportunity, and now Zara had definitely busted her. It was all over. Eve's hard expression spoke volumes.

Goddamn Zara! Now Amelia was doomed, just as predicted. She could feel it in her bones as surely as she could see Eve storming her way.

Jodi came apart on the inside with every step Eve took. Her emotions, her deep connection to Eve, far greater than she could dare admit, were crashing down around her. Every moan of pleasure, every whisper of her name, every detail of personal information they'd shared, had created that connection, long before she laid eyes on Eve. And now her Eve, with her expression void and anger tightening in her jaw, was going to turn her world upside down.

Jodi felt trapped and ashamed.

And now it was too late. It was too late for Eve to hear the truth from Jodi's mouth, too late for Jodi to explain who and what she was for her own personal reasons.

It was too fucking late.

She braced herself for the catfight, for the sting of that delicate hand across her face, and thought of Amelia, how Amelia was right, how the only person going to get hurt was Jodi. Jodi was going to fall apart. How she knew that, she didn't know. The pit of her soul told her so, and then Eve came to a halt in front of her.

"That offer still good?"

Jodi blinked. "Y…yes."

"Meet me outside in five." Eve turned and vanished so quickly that Jodi wasn't sure she'd ever been there.

Jodi turned to Amelia and shrugged. Had she misread Eve's expression? She begged heaven that she had.

Her heart sank. She had to fix this, had to tell Eve. All of it. That she was a sex operator. Eve's sex operator. That she fucked for a fee.

❖

Eve stomped down the sidewalk toward Jodi's condo with Jodi racing to keep stride. As much as she wanted to scream out her rage, she had to keep her cool. Nothing would change the fact that she'd been sleeping with a fucking personal escort.

And now she'd pissed off Zara with her little act of bravado. She knew Zara well enough to know she wouldn't show her face at the final moment just to prove she carried the power to create conflict and cause trouble. To prove to Eve that she needed her as a buyer. As well as the group she brought to every show.

She dug her cell from her purse and dialed Khandi. "I need you to go through the Rolodex and contact every bidder we've ever used. The star design is no longer for sale. It's on the auction block."

"What? Are you serious? What the hell happened?" Khandi yelled.

"It doesn't matter. Get Roger to the suite to help. I want every number dialed before the night's end. I want that dress on every computer screen in every country before it makes it to the runway. Ditch Zara's."

"Am I dreaming? We're really going to be free of the Queen of I Love Myself?"

"Seems that way."

"God, I love you."

Eve almost smiled. "Can you handle it?"

"Pfft. I'm already done."

Eve closed her cell phone and looked straight ahead. She had nothing to say to Jodi as they walked briskly along the sidewalk to her apartment. She should be hurt, but for some reason, she wasn't. She should be angry and violent, but she wasn't that either.

It was too late for pity or anger. She'd been sleeping with a hooker for days. But how was that different from the sex operator she allowed to seduce her nightly? The one she paid to help her come? She wanted to laugh. Somehow, she'd woven herself into a different world from the normal people surrounding her, from the people who had lovers and partners waiting at home.

She couldn't do relationships, nor did she want to, so she'd added a sex operator to speed dial. Now she was sleeping with someone who got paid to fuck.

How ironic was that?

Eve dared a glance at Jodi, who seemed content to allow the quiet walk. What was she thinking? Did she know that Eve knew? What excuses would she have? Or would she have any? In all honestly, she didn't owe Eve an explanation.

Nor did Eve want one.

Right now, she just wanted Jodi's hands on her, around her, in her. She wanted penetrating screams ripped from her throat, wanted Jodi's face between her thighs, wanted her fingers buried deep.

She quickened her steps and Jodi rushed to keep up.

"Is everything okay?"

"It will be as soon as you get me naked." Eve stopped at the entrance to the building and waited for Jodi to key in the code to unlock the doors.

Jodi cleared her throat nervously and led the way across the lobby and into the elevator. Eve focused on the digital readout above the doors, willing it to speed up. Finally, the elevator came to a halt and Eve followed Jodi to her apartment. Jodi closed the door behind them.

Eve kept walking, shedding clothes as she went. Only when she stood naked beside Jodi's bed did she turn around. "Take off your clothes, Jodi."

Hesitantly, Jodi undressed. Eve climbed into the center of the bed, fascinated. Jodi was probably the most gorgeous woman she'd ever encountered. She met and matched all Eve's fantasies and more. That brick-hard body, those captivating green eyes, and that flyaway hair— Jodi had been ripped right out of her mind, her fantasy fuck, piece by lickable piece. She was by far the best fuck Eve had ever had, and she was a damn hooker. She got paid to make women come. Handsomely, by the looks of this condo.

How could that not be fascinating? The fact that women, obviously many of them, kept coming right back to the woman now standing naked before her, waiting, ready for the next command.

Jodi stood her ground. Any movement might break the spell, might slice the ground from under her feet and dump her in the shit.

"Get your toy."

Jodi moved robotically to the nightstand and fastened the dildo around her hips while Eve faced the iron bars. She swallowed when Eve grabbed hold of the top rail and looked over her shoulder, expectation strong on her narrow face, that raven hair like a silk cloak against her back and shoulders.

With emotions tangling inside her, Jodi moved across the bed and between Eve's parted thighs.

"Jodi?"

"Yes?"

"Don't stop until I beg you to."

The order threw Jodi off-key, the softly voiced commands confusing her. She desperately wanted Eve to talk to her, to confirm Jodi's worst suspicion. In the same fleeting thought, she didn't want to ruin the next few hours. She had Eve tonight. That's all that mattered.

She parted Eve's slit with the tip of her finger, slicking through her creaminess, and inhaled her potent arousal. Then she pushed inside her.

Eve whimpered.

Jodi lay over her, pumping deep and slow. She kissed the dragon, trailing a wet path down Eve's spine, across her shoulders, into the crook of her neck. Eve arched, driving herself back, her knuckles white with her death grip on the bars.

"Harder, Jodi."

Jodi leaned back on her knees, wishing she knew what Eve wanted from her, what she expected, what would make her never forget.

Tonight could be her last night before New York called her home.

Was Eve going to let Jodi fuck her and then leave? Was she ever going to talk to Jodi, tell her what was wrong, scream, yell, rant, or rave?

Jodi pulled free of her, grabbed Eve's legs, and jerked her knees out from under her. When Eve turned a startled look on her, Jodi rolled her onto her back and eased between her legs.

Eve opened her mouth to protest, but Jodi halted her with a finger against those lips. "Shh. I haven't let you down yet, have I?"

Eve shook her head.

Jodi eased deeper between Eve's thighs and drew a leg up and over her shoulder.

With a single drive, she entered her.

Eve dug her head into the pillow and clutched at Jodi. Her other foot arched against Jodi's ribs, sliding down to her hip with every upward thrust.

Jodi loved how Eve's lips pursed when she drilled deep, how they parted when she withdrew. She was breathtaking—beautiful and stunning. She was angelic and a lioness all wrapped into one petite little frame.

She pumped faster, stronger, arching deep inside her, then eased down over her.

She drew her bottom lip between her teeth and chewed, sucking the tip of her tongue while Eve moaned, her breathing ragged.

Jodi caressed her rib cage, farther down, over the cheek of her ass, then up the leg draped over her shoulder. She stopped when she reached her ankle and reversed the path. When she reached that firm cheek again, she kept going down, deeper, until she encountered her puckered entrance.

Eve clutched tighter and Jodi pressed her finger against the resisting ring, already slick, ready.

"Please, Jodi."

Jodi flicked her tongue across Eve's top lip. "I like it when you beg, Eve." She drove against her and then pressed her finger harder, lighter, then harder again, pushing in light pulses against her opening.

"God, do it. Jodi, do it."

Jodi slicked her tongue into Eve's mouth at the same time she pressed her finger inside. She swallowed Eve's moan and pumped deep, driving both dildo and finger in the same thrust. In, out, hard, soft, fast, slow, she fucked Eve.

Her whole body quivered against Jodi and then she froze, back arched, head thrown back, and lips parted. "Oh, shit! I'm c-coming!"

Eve thrashed and clutched, one leg clamping around Jodi's and her hips thrusting forward over the dildo.

Jodi never lost stride, riding the wave with her, tortured, as always, by those cries. She closed her eyes.

This would be the last time she ever felt the true impact of that sound.

Chapter Sixteen

Jodi awoke, instantly aware that the warm body she'd spooned all night was missing. She sat up with a start, staring at the hallway light creeping across her bedroom floor. The digital clock on the wall above her closet read 4:03 a.m. The river lights filtered through the open curtains while she gave a heavy sigh. She'd looked forward to waking with Eve in her arms, making love to her one more time, being with Eve as her final day began. Would she be frantic? Rushed? Grouchy and mean? Now she'd never know.

She sighed. Obviously, Eve had alternate thoughts about waking up with Jodi snuggled around her.

She scanned the lighted area of the floor for Eve's clothes, then remembered she'd shed most of them outside the bedroom, starting by the front door.

Had Eve left in the middle of the night? Recently? She felt the empty space beside her. Still warm. She saw the vague outline of something on the pillow and flipped on the bedside lamp. Praying it was a note from Eve, she snatched it up.

Her breath caught and hung in her throat when her fingers closed around a crisp one hundred dollar bill. With shaky hands, she turned it over in her hand.

Keep the change. Bold words scribbled in red lipstick.

Jodi stifled a gasp as the sucker punch ripped through her heart.

A whore. It was true. She was a paid whore, who, until recently, had always held her head high for every decision she'd made throughout her life.

The words reached out from the bill, mocking her, driving home the cold, hard facts of her life. A sidewalk tramp. That's what those red words screamed. The very thing she'd fought against all along. She could have easily been just that, a street hooker, owned by a pimp whose only mercy was her food and the clothing on her back. She would have had a warm bed, a roof over her head, but at what price? Her pride? Her sanity? Her soul? Her life?

She shuddered as the answer swept through her mind. She'd witnessed it—hookers dragged down a back alley by their pimps, kicked and beaten to an immobile state for allowing a john to pass them by. Worse, some had been starved until they begged for death, or they were drugged, daily, hourly, unconscious while their pimps ushered the johns in one at a time.

As quickly as the hurt had swarmed through her veins, anger and rage took hold. Jodi shoved off the bed to kick out the harsh thoughts, wrestling away the image of a hooker stumbling down the street, recently punched by her owner, eyes swollen and purple, lip split and bleeding, desperately, dangerously approaching cars to find a john to please her master. All for a twenty-pound blow job.

I am not a fucking hooker. I am not a fucking whore. I called my own fucking shots. Jodi forked her fingers through her hair as she reeled her emotions back in, taking in deep, calming breaths. She hadn't lived that life. Hadn't been owned by anybody, ridiculed by either pimp or client, or killed. Her johns had been phone voices. Her johns had become successful clients who paid handsomely for her. Her devoted "dates" were still coming back for more, and they paid her price. *Her* price. Not a pimp's.

She took a few steps, slowly calming, until she felt relieved, and thankfully, a few pieces of pride back intact.

"Amelia," Jodi whispered. "Son of a bitch!"

She grabbed her jeans and hopped to her cell phone while jamming her legs in. Her own selfish needs were going to come crashing around her best friend's ears, all for the sake of a fuck, all for the burning need to have Eve release those lonely cries in person.

She speed-dialed Amelia while she searched for her sports bra and shirt, long lost in her desperation to obey Eve's command.

"I have one more hour to sleep, dammit." Amelia's raspy voice filled the line.

"We've got a problem!"

The silence that greeted her was far worse than the tongue-lashing she surely deserved.

"You don't have a fucking problem, Jodi. I do! You just couldn't listen to me, could you?"

"Amelia, I'm sorry. I'll find her and fix this. I swear."

"There's nothing to fix, Jodi. Get off the phone."

Jodi spun around and found Eve standing in the doorway, Jodi's missing button-up shirt hanging like a short gown around her tiny frame, cleavage peeking out against the unbuttoned fold, tan legs begging for Jodi's mouth, and a mug of coffee in each hand.

Jodi forgot her sudden panic as a smile broke across Eve's face.

"Tell Amelia not to worry, that we'll see her in a bit."

Jodi remembered to breathe, to blink.

"I heard. Get off the fucking phone, idiot!" Amelia disconnected the line.

Jodi dropped the phone on the nightstand, still staring, terrified to move and afraid Eve would vanish.

"I see you found my little note?" Eve gave a sultry wink and held out a mug like a peace offering. "Sorry, couldn't resist."

Jodi wasn't sure how to respond when all she wanted to do was knock the steaming liquid from her grasp and spread her out like a Thanksgiving feast. She still wasn't sure if she should be relieved or start begging for Amelia's career. The cat was out of the bag and Eve was still here, prankster or not. Jodi would never admit to her exactly how deep that stab had traveled.

She took the mug and managed a grin.

Eve crawled onto the bed and leaned back against the headboard then pulled her knees to her chest. "So you're a personal escort?"

Jodi wanted to look away, but somewhere in this mix, she had to regain her lifted chin, her confidence, and her pride. Eve didn't walk in her shoes. She never had. Jodi didn't have a reason to hang her head, not a damn reason to be ashamed.

"Yes, I am." Jodi snapped back a little more of that missing pride.

"How does that work, exactly?" Eve looked around the room. "Do you work from a brothel or something? A madam who takes care of all the paperwork?"

"I'm not a whore, Eve. I'm an escort. No brothel. No madam."

"What's the difference? You still fuck for your paycheck, right?"

Jodi chuckled. She had to. Eve's curious expression said she was genuine about the questions and truly wanted the answers. "Yes, as you say, I guess I fuck for a fee."

"How much? Just out of curiosity."

"Does it matter?"

Eve shrugged. "I guess not. But by the looks of your lifestyle, either you charge a pretty penny, or someone really, really likes your company."

"Three thousand."

Eve widened her eyes as she lifted the mug to her lips. "For the night?"

"An hour."

Eve sputtered and pushed off the headboard. She coughed, then cleared her throat. "Holy—Are you serious?" She shook her head and settled back against the bars. "I'm in the wrong line of work."

"Why are you here, Eve?"

Hurt flashed across Eve's eyes and Jodi had the impulse to crawl across her flesh. "Do you want me to leave?"

"No, that's not what I meant. Why did you come here last night? If you knew?"

Eve smiled, her teeth bright over the rim of the navy blue porcelain mug. "Isn't that obvious?"

Jodi matched her grin and nodded, though she didn't much like the answer. Then again, she wasn't sure what answer she'd been expecting.

"We all have our dirty little secrets, Jodi." Eve took a sip. "Including me."

Jodi lay on her side and propped her head in her hand. "Tell me."

Eve put her mug on the nightstand and wiggled down the bed until she was facing Jodi. "I have a sex phone operator on speed dial."

Jodi perked up. She was that person. Lexi was the privileged one to have a spot on Eve Harris's electronic device, her instant link. At the same time, her gut churned. Another secret she was keeping from Eve, another sheltered lie. As much as she wanted to, there were only so many truths she could part with today. If she told Eve, Eve would flee. Of this, she was sure.

"Really now?" Jodi tapped her nose. "The bossy beauty has phone sex? With a stranger?"

Eve rolled onto her back. "I do. And she's addicting. Perfect, in fact."

"Perfect how?" Jodi took shallow breaths, afraid the sound would shut out Eve's answer. That answer was the key to everything. Eve's heart, her soul, all of the unanswered questions, possibly the reason Jodi came undone every time Eve cried her name, were in those answers.

"I...don't know." Eve's expression darkened as she concentrated on the ceiling. "She knows me, inside and out. Yet she knows nothing about me at all. Is that weird?" She turned to look at Jodi. "Hell yes, that's weird."

She turned her focus back on the ceiling while Jodi waited for her to continue, desperate for her confession. "Her voice does something to me. Something no one else has ever done. I can't stop thinking about her, wondering what she's doing, who she's doing. That sexy British accent...jeez, it's so fucking orgasmic."

"As in London?"

Eve nodded. "So you see, I'm not much different from your cli— dates."

"Does she know you're here? Have you ever met?" Jodi probed further, reaching for the answers Eve couldn't express.

"Hell no." Eve scoffed as if that were the most ridiculous thing. "Why would I want to do that? My life's perfect. Career, money, family, and sex on speed dial. I have the elusive fantasy tucked in my cell phone. No bullshit relationships. Reality destroys everything."

Jodi was so shocked at the confession that she rolled onto her back and scooted against Eve. It had never occurred to her that Eve, or anyone for that matter, thought about her, what she was doing, where she was going, if she was fucking another. It also saddened her to know that Eve found their link perfect, that the link would never evolve past that point. The fantasy was all that Eve wanted, nothing beyond that.

What the fuck was she thinking? Her clients were just that, clients. She didn't want relationships with them either. Well, until Eve. Eve had struck deep and fast, drawing out emotions Jodi never knew existed.

"Don't you ever want a real relationship?" Jodi was beginning to wonder if she was the only hopeless romantic on earth. Here she was, a paid escort who wouldn't allow a woman to touch her who was picking up the check, or paying for sex. Yet she held strong to the hope of love, believing that it would find her, that it would shake her ground and hook her for life.

"Aren't you cute?" Eve rolled onto her side. "You're one of those? Waiting for Ms. Right? The picket fence, the furry dog, cars in the garage, and three point two kids?"

Jodi didn't want to answer. But she had to. "Yes. I guess I'm one of them." She pulled Eve on top of her. "I want a pretty little thing like you to come home to me every night." She kissed her lips. "To make love to me before bedtime, do it again before we go to work, and even on my lunch break." She kissed her cheek. "To hold my hand while we stroll through the park." She kissed her neck. "To walk with me in the rain."

Eve stiffened and Jodi knew she'd gone too far.

"What the hell is it with women and the damn rain lately?" Eve grabbed Jodi's hand and folded it around her breast. "Before you fuck me again, I have one more question."

Jodi ducked and licked a stiff nipple. "Ask away."

"Why didn't you tell me?" Eve arched back and offered her other breast.

"Amelia. I couldn't risk her career." Jodi pulled the hardened flesh into her mouth and gave a gentle chew. "She's worked her ass off to get here. I couldn't forgive myself if I fucked that up for her."

Eve released that raw moan and Jodi fastened her mouth around her nipple and sucked, pumping her hips up against Eve.

"One more question."

Jodi moved back to the first breast and sucked the tip into her mouth.

"Why me, Jodi?"

With a loud pop of disconnection from her suctioned hold, Jodi glanced up at her. She couldn't answer. Like Eve, she didn't know the answer. God, how she wished she did.

Slowly, she rolled Eve onto her back and wedged herself between her thighs. "Because I knew your whimpers would be too erotic to miss."

If Eve only knew how many times she'd heard those erotic cries. How many times they'd almost broken her down.

❖

Eve rushed into her hotel room and searched for Khandi, giving a sigh of relief when she found all rooms vacant. With the coast clear, Eve undressed and fell on the bed with her cell phone. Surely Lexi would answer this time of the morning. She had the first day Eve arrived in London. Please let her today. She needed to hear her familiar voice.

"Good morning, my beautiful Eve," Lexi answered, her sexy accent instantly awakening Eve's lust.

"Where the hell have you been, sexy?" Eve stretched out, not caring that she only had an hour to shower, dress, and get her ass to the studio. Today, she just couldn't care. Though Khandi would flip into panic mode in one hour and one minute. Roger would hover on the edge of a coronary in one hour and three minutes.

"Had a bit of a family emergency. All is well now. I see you're calling early again. Are your people raking those feisty nerves again?"

Eve smiled and hugged the phone to her ear. God, how she'd missed Lexi, missed the way she knew how to coax Eve to calmness and to an intense orgasm, almost always in the same phone call.

"No. But give them time. I leave for work soon." Eve fanned her hands down her stomach and curled her palm against her crotch, surprised how wet she was. She'd just come by Jodi's hands half the night, and again half the wee hours of the morning, yet Lexi's voice stirred her need like no one else.

Well, except Jodi. Lexi she could tuck away and use on demand. Jodi, she was too real.

"What are you wearing, Eve?"

"Nothing. Absolutely nothing."

"I like that. Are you alone?"

"Completely."

"Splendid. Put me on speakerphone. You'll need your hands free."

Eve pushed the speaker button and laid the phone between her breasts. "Done."

"First, I want you to let everything loose. Arms out to the side, legs straight out. Relax."

Eve did as told, never questioning Lexi's tactics. Her ways didn't matter; the ending result was always the same. Eve coming, hard.

"Close your eyes, Eve. See me. The image I've described to you."

She tried. God, how she tried. Only problem was, Jodi was all she could see now. Jodi also had green eyes, the same as Lexi had told her she possessed. Jodi also had a sexy, grooved tummy, the very one Lexi had described in great detail. Jodi had that un-groomed hair that Eve had fisted in her grasp all week.

"That person, the one you see so clear in your mind, is going to make you come…through your fingers."

"Yes. Make me come, Lexi."

"My mouth is your fingers. Your fingers are mine. Touch yourself, Eve."

Eve moved her hand between her legs and curved her fingers over her pussy. "Yes. Shit, yes. I'm wet. You make me so wet, J—Lexi."

"I'm moving down your body, sucking, licking, tasting every inch of you. Dropping between those parted thighs."

Eve inhaled sharply as Jodi's face materialized, those eyes steady on Eve with her descent between her thighs before latching on to her, sucking, and driving those fingers deep.

She opened her eyes and concentrated on the face she once envisioned. Darker green eyes. Shorter hair. Lexi.

"I can taste you, Eve. You are sweet on my tongue. I'm going to drink every drop of you."

Once again, she closed her eyes, holding tight to the Lexi she always imagined, and spread her lips apart, touching herself, flicking and circling.

Lexi's mouth worked against her inner thighs, teasing, never touching her clit, her hot breath light puffs against her flesh. Eve gave in to the images, relaxing, back in familiar, safe, territory with Lexi's voice. Her fingers curled inside and then Jodi was hovering over her, her face void of emotion, driving her pussy down hard on Eve's leg. She was grinding, her fingers surging against a place that no other woman had touched before. Eve had never come so hard in her life, the orgasm running rampant through every part of her body in reckless waves.

She huffed and opened her eyes.

Once again, she drove the image of Jodi away, desperate for Lexi's face to root itself instead.

"What's wrong, my sweet thing?"

"Nothing. Keep talking." Eve let her eyes flutter shut and flicked faster. "Seduce me, Lexi."

"Can you feel me, Eve? Latched on? Sucking? Drinking you?"

Eve grabbed a tight hold to Lexi's virtual reality. She lifted her hips from the bed and drove two fingers inside herself, frantically circling against her clit, afraid Jodi would appear again.

In the second it took her to inhale, Jodi was there, back again, staring at her naked reflection through the glass, pumping her fingers deep then dragging them over her clit. She lifted her hood while Eve looked back at her. Then she drove herself inside.

"Shit!" Eve bolted upright. "Lexi. I'm so sorry. I have to go."

She hung up, chunked the phone on the floor, and then shoved off the bed. "What the fuck?"

Eve stood behind the curtain as each model made her way down the catwalk. Flashes erupted from beyond the sheer material from inside the theater as photographers took their customary shots.

She felt overwhelmed and enlivened, both with the success of another event, even without Zara's presence. The bitch hadn't shown up, just as Eve predicted. Smart thinking had any loss of sales taken care of. The auction was under way for the star design, even as the models turned and posed for the audience. Bids had already reached well over two hundred thousand. Eve smiled. Before the night ended, her hair-pulling design could very well be worth a million dollars. It had been a risky decision, one she hadn't hesitated to make, and now that decision was paying off. To hell with Zara and her fat bank account. She didn't fucking need her. No more putting up with Zara's abnormal obsession with herself or that egotistical bravado. She was completely done with the likes of her.

Right now, all she had to concern herself with was every model making it down the runway without tripping over platform shoes or top-siding a heavy headpiece, and then she could celebrate the end of hell week, in Jodi's bed.

Tonight would be the last time she saw Jodi, the last time she would have the pleasure of coming by her hands. She wouldn't seek her out next year, or any year, for that matter. It ended tonight. Of course, she'd never forget her, or the person she was, or the personal things they'd shared with each other. She wasn't ashamed of their time together. At all. They'd opened up to each other. Neither would use those secrets against the other.

Of course, no one close to Eve would care or be shocked, but she could well imagine the press would have a field day with such juicy tidbits about a phone sex operator. They could possibly go so far as to drag her mystery woman out of hiding. God forbid.

She hadn't stopped thinking about Lexi from the second she chunked her cell phone aside, unable to have an orgasm, unable to kick the sight of Jodi from her mind. That had never happened before. Even their first phone call had ended with Eve climaxing, that voice seducing her, pushing her into the erotic moment. So why now? Work overload? The fact that all week she'd come more times than should be humanly possible?

Eve knew that wasn't the answer. Lexi did things to her no one else could, or had. She wasn't ashamed to admit that Lexi fit perfectly into her chaotic world, that Lexi was perfect for her in every way. Lexi jerked her out of the tension with her soothing words. Lexi was all she needed. All she wanted. All she would ever have, and she wanted to keep it that way. Forever.

Even the cold shower hadn't helped, though she'd masturbated without failure minutes after, with Jodi vivid in her thoughts, sucking her, driving into her. The feel of her hands, the way she pulled throaty groans out of Eve. Lord help her, she was damn good at her job. Jodi was in the right profession, for sure. And Eve had been the center of her world for days.

Or had she been?

Her insides cramped once again, bringing that little green monster to life, same as it had done all morning just thinking about the things Jodi most likely did to her clients. She huffed at her own weakness as the last model stepped beside her wearing the very gown that had nearly made her tear the hair from her head. The one in the middle of an auction war right now.

Black and crimson, lying delicately against the model's lean figure, was her reality in living color, the very reason she worked her fingers to the bone. Her precious designs. She held her breath as tears threatened, and thought of her mother, how she'd never put anything above her daughter or her husband, how she'd treasured, cherished, her family.

Eve had this—work, career, long, grueling hours—and nothing else. Nothing. Not even a damn dog to wag a tail when she walked through the door. Not a lover, a partner, or a best friend. Void. Her life was void of the important things. The very things Jodi, a paid fucking escort, wanted above all else. A hopeless romantic trapped in her own career, waiting patiently for love to snatch her from her life.

How pathetic. How sad.

They were polar opposites.

Applause broke out and Eve snapped to attention. The model U-turned at the end of the runway, her face blank, expressionless, model-perfect, then she slipped behind the curtain and walked back stage.

The applause held while Eve stepped onto the stage and looked out over the crowd lined around the runway. She never walked the aisle like some designers did. That space was for the models, and she'd never take any credit from them.

She waved and found Jodi sitting among the people, the slouched posture and cool expression that made Eve a little loopy, those penetrating eyes undressing every inch of her.

Her stomach fluttered and her neck burned with a blush.

CHAPTER SEVENTEEN

Eve pushed her plate away, the food half-eaten. The fashion show, and the week, had come to a conclusion, completely successful. The room she'd reserved for the finale dinner was crowded and filled with excitement, overflowing with high-spirited chatter from the crew, including Jodi and Amelia, who talked mainly to each other.

She should be beside herself with excitement, yet all she could think about was Lexi, how she wanted to hear her voice, tell her she was sorry for cutting their call short.

What she wanted more than anything was privacy so Lexi could coax her to that promised orgasm, to the one Eve had failed to achieve. She wasn't sure what she was more upset about—the fact that Jodi had invaded her mind during her personal time with Lexi, or the fact that Lexi's voice couldn't overshadow Jodi's face.

She instinctively looked Jodi's way. Jodi gave a single nod and a timid smile fell across her lips. Gorgeous. Perfect in every way. Well, besides that little thing about being an escort. But who the hell cared? Eve sure didn't. She wasn't there to judge or ridicule. God knew she had her own messed-up life.

She returned the smile while Lexi's voice hummed in the back of her mind. She needed to call her, to finish. If for nothing else, for her self-assurance that hell week had been the logical reason behind her inability to climax, that even though she'd successfully masturbated minutes later, it was only a one-time fluke.

Lexi was her perfect commitment. Nothing could change that.

She rose and tapped her fork against her wine glass, needing freedom from the British accent scrambling quickly to the surface of her mind.

Everyone hushed and looked her way. "Every fashion show seems to get better than the last, and this one was no exception. Everything ran impeccably, and the outcome proved how hard you all worked to make this show a success. I'm so proud to call you my employees, my friends, and my family."

Cheers and claps filled the room. She'd done it, pulled off another event without any flaws or fuck-ups. She should be ecstatic. Instead, anxiety and confusion took hold.

Eve looked to Amelia and motioned for her to stand. Amelia hesitantly pushed her chair back. Eve held her wine glass in the air. "I'd like to formally introduce Amelia, owner of Ruccar and the artist who provided us with those beautiful props this year."

Once again, everyone clapped while Amelia smiled and nodded to the ones nearest her.

"If you're up for the challenge for more hell weeks, I'd be honored to welcome you aboard our chaotic little family. Permanently."

Amelia gasped and threw her hand over her mouth, tears welling in her eyes. She nodded as Jodi stood and wrapped her in a bear hug.

Eve studied them with a mixture of longing and loneliness. How would this new change affect Jodi? Her only true friend would soon be traveling near and far, caught up in a whirlwind of fashion events, with little time to be together. Yet something deep within told her Amelia and Jodi could and would survive anything, that this new fork in the road would only enhance their unbreakable bond.

The chatter increased again as everyone moved around to greet Amelia with hugs and handshakes, then they hugged each other.

Eve appraised her employees, her family, and then downed the contents of her wine glass. The urge to call Lexi only increased with every passing hug, every clap on the back. The need to hear her voice was consuming.

She made her way into the bar area, if anything, to catch a breath of fresh air. She was on edge when she should be calm. She was nervous when there was no need to be. She was feeling lonely in a room packed with familiar faces and that confused her more than anything. She never felt lonely or alone. There was never a dull moment in her day or a time when people weren't swarming all around her. How could she be lonely when her life was so full and perfect? Just the way she'd sketched it out all those years ago.

Lexi. She needed to call Lexi. Her voice, her soothing words, would fix this. It always did.

Missing everything about Lexi, desperate to wrap herself inside her voice, Eve found a vacant stool and ordered a refill. How could she possibly miss a woman she didn't even know? Who was nothing more than a voice on the other end of the line? She could be all the things Eve assumed. So how could she still pine for her? Need her? Was it the fact that Lexi knew her deepest sexual fantasies and wielded them for Eve during every call?

Jodi's face sparked to life. Gorgeous, with those striking eyes. She was a gentleman. A lover of life, and a lover to a hundred women. In flesh form, she'd given Eve her fantasies. Those deep, dark secrets only Lexi knew of. Not only that, she'd made Eve think about friends and family. Shit. She'd made her think of love.

What the hell was she thinking? Jodi didn't make her think of those things. Something had, for sure, but not Jodi. Well, maybe she had a little. The birthday party with silly balloons and lots of laughter. Holding her hand during their walk along the Thames, the comforting feeling and the calmness of normalcy. The way she'd worked Eve's body into submission, the way Lexi did over the wire.

Eve shook her head in confusion. She fingered the rim of her glass and thought about her week. She'd spent ample time with Jodi. Yet she thought of Lexi almost every minute. Lexi might not be real, or rather, in living color, but she was all Eve had ever wanted. She was all Eve needed to fulfill her life. She was her perfect commitment.

How was it possible for a fucking voice to be her everything, everything that completed her spitfire world? It was sick. She knew that. Yet nothing could stop the tidal wave of need coiling inside her with the thought of Lexi, the need to dial her number right that second, to curl herself around that phone and just listen, soaking in every deep syllable.

Shit! She was seriously disturbed.

She was in love with a fucking voice.

"Has she seemed unusually quiet tonight? Are you sure she was okay with your...profession?" Amelia asked as they stepped out onto the sidewalk to talk away from the crowd. Concern was evident in her voice, though the smile hadn't faded from her face after Eve's speech.

Jodi was so proud of her. She also hated that any part of her life would put a crimp in Amelia's night, in her well-fought-for joy.

"Don't worry about that right now. You have a new career to think about. All those exotic places you'll be traveling to." As soon as the words left Jodi's mouth, she felt isolated and detached. Amelia would be gone and Jodi would be here with her "dates," filling her little black book, widening her itinerary.

She wouldn't have Amelia for lunch dates or spa treatments or late-night drinks at their favorite pub. Her life was going to change with Amelia's, but in a whole different way.

Amelia would be living her dream, while Jodi became someone else's fantasy.

Jodi could feel her departure already, though she wouldn't dare admit that to Amelia. She missed her already.

"What will you do?"

Jodi thought. What else could she do? "I might take up a little traveling of my own. Go out and see a bit of this big bad world. Who knows, maybe I'll show up at one of your fashion events." She winked.

"I feel guilty for some reason. Like I'm abandoning you."

Jodi pulled her into a hug. "Don't you dare feel guilty. I wouldn't trade places with you for anything in the world." She pulled back. "Your new boss is going to work your damn ass off."

Amelia laughed. "God, don't I know it. I hope I can keep up."

An image of Eve flashed through Jodi's mind—Eve charging across the studio the first day she'd laid eyes on her, strutting on those pathetic boots. Jodi had witnessed the workhorse at full speed.

Jodi had had all day to think about her, about their conversation, how she needed to tell Eve the truth.

Eve's phone call with "Lexi" was even more reason. Eve had been different, changed somehow. Something had been wrong. Eve hadn't climaxed. Though Jodi found a little pleasure in the fact, hoping she was the reason.

Yet there was something else, something hidden beneath Eve's pleas for Jodi to keep talking, to keep coaxing her toward orgasm. Still, Eve hadn't reached satisfaction.

Was Jodi to blame?

She'd wanted Eve to see her face when she closed her eyes. Had prayed for it. What if Eve had had a sudden realization that she didn't need Lexi any longer? What if her calls stopped coming? What if Lexi never heard from Eve again?

She shifted uneasily to her other foot. To top off all insecurities, why had Eve turned to Lexi so fast after leaving her bed? The question nagged her more than anything, the fact that she hadn't been enough for Eve, that Eve still needed something more in someone else, something she obviously hadn't gotten from Jodi.

Eve was special. She'd known it all along. Now her profession was out in the open, and Eve had stayed. She knew that Jodi had bedded hundreds of women, thickening her pockets fuck after fuck. Yet she'd stayed. She hadn't cared.

What if Eve was the one? What if she was the one that Jodi would never forget? The one she'd never rip from her mind? The one she already couldn't wrestle from her thoughts? Hadn't her soul been telling her something all along? Through every phone call, listening to Eve's sweet cries?

It was Eve. It always had been.

Jodi stuffed her hands in her pockets and looked through the glass, straining to find Eve in the crowd. She found her perched at the bar. She was so beautiful. Jodi wanted her like she'd wanted nothing else in her life. She couldn't look away as coworkers stopped to hug her. Though she returned the smile, there was something missing in her expression. Life?

When the group moved away, Eve pushed off the stool and dissolved into the darkest corner of the bar, where the shadows swallowed her.

"What are you going to do about her?"

"Nothing. I'm not going to do anything." But she was, and she knew it. God, she was going to fuck up. She turned back to Amelia. "I don't know what to do."

She'd just tell her the truth. What did she have to lose? If she didn't take a chance now, she'd never know, even if that chance never took her anywhere at all. Eve deserved to know. She needed to know that the person she sought for sexual relief was Jodi.

But how? When? It would have to be perfect. But what was perfect? When was the right time? She prayed her instincts would let her know.

Amelia shrugged, but sympathy danced in her eyes.

Jodi's sex line chirped, that distinct ring tone that belonged to only Eve.

Amelia looked down at the phone while Jodi panicked. She shoved around and strained to see Eve in the darkness. She was there, back pressed against the booth, chair pulled protectively in front of her, completely out of eyeshot to anyone strolling past the bar area.

When Jodi turned back to Amelia, fear withering through her veins, Amelia rolled her eyes playfully as only Amelia could and walked back inside.

Jodi inhaled deeply, took a careful glance around her to make sure she was alone, and then flipped open the cell phone, simultaneously dropping her voice into the British accent that drove Eve to whimpers.

"Hello, my sexy."

"Lexi." Eve's voice was light and rushed. "I need you to listen."

"Mmm. I think I might like this." Jodi stepped away from the window and pressed herself against the brick building.

"Something has...I have to tell you...fuck!" Eve took a deep breath.

"Relax, Eve. What's wrong?"

"I can't...Lexi?"

"Yes, Eve? Tell me what's on your mind."

"I can't stop thinking about you."

"I like knowing you think about me. What are you wearing, Eve?"

"No!" Eve sighed. "Like, ever. Always, you're on my mind."

Jodi moved back to the window. Eve was still in the gray shadows, the phone pulled protectively against her ear, a watchful eye on the crowd.

"I think I'm addicted to you, Lexi."

Eve wanted her. But was it Jodi, the real person behind the Brit accent? Or Lexi? Dammit, they were one and the same. No matter what number Eve dialed, it was always Jodi on the other end. Always Jodi in charge. It was Jodi's words, through every fake accent, that dragged Eve into her erotic state of mind.

It had always been Jodi. Or had it? She couldn't tell what Eve wanted. Did she want the fantasy with no strings attached? Or did she want to take a chance on her living fantasy?

Jodi fisted her hand against her scalp and struggled for the answer, for the right thing to do. Telling Eve could fuck up everything, especially the only tie she had left to her, that damn phone. But not telling her. It was going to tear Jodi apart.

She blew out a breath. This was her chance and she knew it. With her heart sputtering out of control, she stepped back inside the restaurant and stalled in the lobby, staring toward a woman she could possibly love. A woman she knew she loved. Possibly had all along.

Trained on Eve's dim figure, she no longer wanted this life. This profession. The dates, the money, the little black book, or red carpets.

Normal. She wanted to be normal. The house, fence, kids, and the fucking dog. She could have it, and she deserved it.

"How can I want nothing more than your voice for the rest of my life? How can you be so perfect for me?"

Jodi found a quiet spot against the interior windows, out of the pathway to the exit. She turned her back on Eve and pressed her head against the glass. "Tell me your dreams, Eve."

"You are my dream. A dream come true. I don't want relationships. The chaos relationships bring. I just want you, and this phone, your voice. Is that insane?"

Jodi stiffened, the wind knocked from her lungs. Eve would never want her. She was real, not a fantasy. She couldn't tuck Jodi away when she didn't fit inside her life, then pull her out when her adrenaline high needed to be deflated. The fantasy, it was all Eve wanted. It's all she had ever wanted.

Eve curved tighter over her legs and pressed the phone closer. She wanted to reach through the phone to caress that voice, those lips. God, it was ripping at her, this need, this want. It wasn't normal and she knew it, yet she couldn't stop herself. Desperate. She was desperate. And she wanted nothing more than what she had right this second, her life fulfilled, with Lexi only a phone call away.

Above all else, she wanted to prove to herself that Lexi was still the elusive fantasy, that Jodi's face appearing in her mind, flinging Lexi's image aside, was a fluke, that Lexi could still satisfy her, in every way. That the bullshit dancing in her mind, of mothers and sweet moments, of a house she shared with another, or having a kiss waiting for her at the end of a hectic day. Those thoughts were for her mother. Not Eve! Nor did she want to think about them anymore. She didn't do normal. What she did, she was doing right now. Waiting for Lexi to make her come so she could dive back into what she knew best. Fashion.

She had to get back on track and get her shit together.

With a quick scan around the bar to prove she'd tucked herself far out of sight, she pushed another chair around to block all view of her lower body. "Make me come, Lexi. Right here. Right now."

There was a long pause while Eve slid her hands between her legs. She caressed herself through her slacks, her crotch hot, ready.

"Do it, Lexi." Eve slipped her hand inside her pants and pushed her fingers against her wet slit, dipping lower until her fingers were coated.

"What are you wearing, Eve?"

Eve pressed the tip of her finger against her clit, then flicked, widening her legs. "Black slacks. White silk thong. Hurry. God, hurry." Eve looked out over the expanse of the room, flicking fast against her clit, frantic to come, and spotted Jodi facing the lobby windows, her head angled, one hand pressed to the opposite side of her face.

Dear God, not again! First her visions, now the reality.

She looked fuckable in her gray slacks, and the damn shirt that was obviously one size too small. Always. Dammit, couldn't the woman find a shirt that didn't slick across her body like a lover's tongue?

Eve looked away, determined Jodi wouldn't fit into this phone call. Not this time.

She circled harder and summoned Lexi's image to the surface. "Make me see you, Lexi. No one else. Just…you."

Jodi flinched with her words, how they cut like a razor blade. She'd been a moron to think that maybe, just maybe, Eve could want anything outside her perfect little fantasy world.

From this day forward, every time Eve dialed her number, she'd see that petite body, feel and taste her. Jodi had had her fantasy pumping beneath her. Yet the fantasy was all Eve would ever want, would ever make room for in her life.

Her world was full, packed with all she would need in life, and Jodi could never be part of that world. Lexi could, of course, but not Jodi. The truth slammed hard.

It was time to finish this. Time to walk away, to leave Eve behind in her little sheltered cocoon.

Jodi was done.

First, she had to get the hell out of this building, out of Eve's life. She'd never know about Lexi. She'd make sure of that.

She moved to the door to slip away, to fade into the night so Eve would never have to look back. She'd toss the phone into the nearest trash bin and never have to hear that ring tone again, or Eve's plaintive cries shortly after. If Eve wanted a fantasy, she'd have to find it elsewhere.

A man and woman shoved through the door just as Jodi reached for the handle, their laughter loud. She pulled away to hide the sound of the noise as they raced across the small foyer and into the bar area.

Jodi turned to barrel through the doors and took one last glance in Eve's direction. Eve was watching her, brow angled. She looked to the couple and then back to Jodi.

Jodi couldn't move.

"Say my name." Eve rose from her chair, her expression threatening, confused, and almost pleading.

It was too late for Jodi to move, too late to run. She didn't much care right now. Eve was never hers. Never had been. Eve belonged to her fantasy world, just the way she liked it.

Eve moved in front of the table. Her head swam with confusion, with denial. The way Jodi was staring at her, the phone pressed snug against her ear, she didn't have to hear her name. She needed to hear it.

"Fucking say my name." A sob trapped itself deep in her chest.

Jodi wasn't moving. Standing stock-still, those gorgeous eyes penetrating Eve with the answer.

Eve fisted her hand by her side, her stomach rolling. "Say it, Godammit!"

"I'm Lexi."

Eve watched in horror as Jodi's lips moved, as she both heard and saw the words. "No. Dear God, no." Angry tears sprang to her eyes.

The accent was gone. In its place was that sexy country drawl she'd been hearing all week, feathering commands against her ear, prickling her flesh with their soft breath.

An unsure smile broke across Jodi's lips as if she'd turned Eve's world from shit to gold.

Eve willed herself to stand and not run. Every fiber of her being ignited with the punch of Jodi's confession. Her fantasy, the most perfect sexual connection she'd ever had with another living soul, a woman who knew her deepest, darkest sexual fantasies, was standing within fifty feet of her. The living reality she didn't want in her life.

Something stabbed with harsh force, the realization of her entire week with Jodi. "You've known all along? The whole time?"

Jodi nodded but held her expression firm. "From the second you spoke your first words in the studio. I'd know your voice anywhere."

Tears welled in Eve's eyes. She couldn't look away, couldn't feel a thing. Her whole body was numb, her mind void. She felt like someone had drained her, had ripped her soul clear from her body until she was empty. Boneless. She felt boneless as Jodi stood motionless.

She'd never had such an absolute connection to anyone, let alone someone clear across the world, or on a damn phone. Somehow, someway, she'd found that connection, had clutched at it like a security blanket.

Depression swarmed around her like a cold, black wind.

Eve shook her head and took a step back until she bumped the table. "I trusted you. Trusted Lexi…you. The things I said. Things we did." She tightened her grip against the rush of tears. "You betrayed me."

Jodi took a step forward, hating the hurt and fragile expression, as if she had physically punched Eve. In honesty, she guessed she had. She was deflating Eve's bubbled world, where everything was the way Eve saw fit, no blemishes. Where Eve had her reality and her fantasy all wrapped into a neat little package. Where nothing and no one could touch or change it.

As much as she wanted to race across the room and pull Eve against her, stroke the hair back from her face, and beg her forgiveness, there was nothing she could do to change this outcome.

Eve had already spelled it out in black and white.

Jodi drew in a breath, her heart already missing the sound of Eve's voice. "I can't be your fantasy, Eve. I've already been your reality."

With one last look at the face she wouldn't soon forget, she turned and slipped out the glass doors. She shoved the phone deep in her pocket and kicked up her steps. Far away. She needed to get far away from Eve.

She didn't stop her fast pace until she got to the middle of Westminster Bridge.

The lights twinkled and sparkled, reflecting like a dark impressionist landscape in the water. She loved this spot, the beautiful skyline, the quiet and serenity. A place she would have never known if not for her mother's desperate need to mend her broken heart, to start a new life. Jodi had been paying the price ever since.

Jodi had walked every alley of this city, run as if the hounds of hell were after her through most of them. She knew it inside and out—where to score drugs, where the pedophiles lurked, usually with their hand jerking in their pants, where not to venture if her life depended on it, ever. She knew the vendors, most by name, who would share, who wouldn't dare.

She leaned her forearms against the railing. The water drifted lazily. She thought of her father. What an incredible man he'd been. Protective and stern, so in love with his family. He'd made a gentleman out of his only child. She thought of her mother, how loving she'd been, how in love she'd been with Jodi's father. Jodi had adopted her faithfulness, her undying need to love and be loved. She thought of her life, her past, but most of all, she thought of Eve.

Jodi wasn't the twisted one. Eve was.

With a silent prayer that Eve would find all her heart desired, that Jodi would find love herself, she held the phone to her lips, closed her eyes against a silent prayer, then flipped Lexi's only connection to Eve into the Thames.

CHAPTER EIGHTEEN

Eve dropped into the desk chair and avoided looking at her computer, focusing on the windows stretched against the outer wall of her office instead. Beyond the glass was a bleary, overcast day, very much matching her mood of late.

The normal get-up-and-go girl couldn't find the oomph to get up and go anymore. She was still doing her job, as always. She'd expect nothing less of herself. But it was getting harder to find her day-to-day drive, the spark that normally kept her on her toes, in control.

She couldn't shake off her lethargy, the feeling she refused to call depression. She'd tried, really, she had.

Six months had passed her by, and what had she achieved other than spending every waking moment throwing herself headlong into sketches and designs, models and itineraries? No matter how far she sank into her career, the anxiety was right with her, working alongside her, breathing down her neck. Even the creation of another breathtaking design hadn't tugged her from the black hole.

She'd been duped, deceived. Lied to. By a woman she trusted. Trusted with her heart, her secrets, her fantasies. She kept telling herself over and over that no one knew, and that no one cared even if they did know, but even that didn't make the knife in her back feel any less painful.

Betrayed. That's how she felt. Completely and utterly betrayed.

Lexi. Jodi.

Eve shook her head and finally turned her attention to the monitor. She had to stop this nonsense. All this thinking. It was fucking with her mind. The drama was over. Over and done.

Pink memo slips were stacked dead center on her keyboard as a reminder that she had urgent messages. A hundred e-mails would be in her inbox, just as they always were. Some would get forwarded to Khandi without reading the body; some she'd save for later. The rest would be sent to the trash bin.

Every day, same start. Day after day after day.

Worse, she hadn't stopped looking for an e-mail from Jodi. God only knew why. What could Jodi possibly say to erase the fact that she'd lied, that she'd omitted all truths, that she'd made a complete mockery of Eve's confession? God, the things Eve had told her, how she was addicted to a phone voice, to the things that voice commanded her to do to herself. Jodi knew the deepest part of her, the part that belonged to no one else but herself. She knew, and she'd allowed Eve to carry on.

Eve felt like a fool. Yet she couldn't stop thinking about Jodi. The visual image of her was strong, even after all these months. Their long walk along the river, rain falling all around them, Jodi holding her hand, how warm and comfy and protected she'd felt. Every minute of their time had been a lie. And for once in Eve's life, she'd put aside her dying devotion to her career. For once, she hadn't cared that work awaited. For once, she'd lost herself in their time together, in those eyes, in her bed. And it'd been amazing. Every minute of it.

With an aggravated grunt, Eve shoved the to-do notes aside and opened her in-box. Might as well get something done. Everything else might feel dead, but her career, she'd worked too long and too hard to let anything screw that up.

Khandi breezed into the office and slammed the door shut behind her, startling Eve. She walked to the desk holding a stack of magazines, her face set and determined.

"Look, I have to tell you something, and you're going to be pissed, but hopefully you'll still love me and buy me nice bonus gifts, like the Gucci bag last Christmas that I loved, as you know, oh, and that cute little scarf from Macy's that matches my—"

Eve snapped her fingers to speed up the outburst. "Khandi, get to the point before you hyperventilate."

"Okay. See, I know something, something I shouldn't know, but I know, and I should have told you, and, well, I just couldn't cause you were all tongue hanging out your mouth like never before, and, well, I'd never seen you act so gooey-eyed before—"

"Khandi! Seriously! Get to it!"

"Stop yelling at me! You know it makes me all nervous and then I can't think straight, and then I can't remember what I was saying."

"As opposed to the way you're acting now *without* me yelling at you?" Eve studied her more carefully. "You're on the damn cold meds again, aren't you? Seriously, Khandi, you have to read the directions."

Khandi gave her a scowl. "No, Ms. Moody, I'm not on freaking cold medicine."

"Then can you just say whatever it is you're attempting to say and failing miserably at? Please?"

"Here!" Khandi tossed a magazine on the desk.

Eve rolled her eyes. Khandi was going to try her patience to the max with the damn gossip columns. She was sick to death of seeing them, finding them, knowing the contents stemmed from a place she wanted to forget about right now. Eve was going to come unglued soon.

"Just flippin' read the damn thing!"

Eve cocked a warning brow at her and leaned forward. Carlotta Tate, some mastermind producer with the London Theater, dominated the cover.

Eve shrugged and looked up. "And?"

Khandi's expression turned soft and apologetic. "I'm sorry, Eve. She's an escort. There, I said it." She dropped into the chair opposite Eve and blew out a breath.

"Carlotta Tate?"

"No, marble brain. Jodi!"

Eve's heart slammed at the mention of her name. She looked back down at the cover for a closer inspection and found Jodi standing on the edge of the red carpet, face stern, posture straight and stiff in her black tuxedo.

That explained why Khandi had been hoarding all the damn tabloids, leaving them lying around the hotel suite for Eve to stumble upon in London. Then practically begging her to "read this article about Carlotta Tate" and "would you just look at this hottie."

Eve had only herself to blame for ignoring Khandi's reluctance to spill the truth. She instantly wondered if it would have changed her mind had she known, if Khandi had told her instead of beating around the bush. Fact was, she'd been almost desperate to get to Jodi's bed. Knowing those facts probably wouldn't have stopped her either.

Khandi dropped another magazine beside the first. This one bore another female Eve didn't recognize, younger than the last, far more beautiful. She was possessively perched on Jodi's arm, hand tucked around that tight bicep Eve had had the pleasure of licking, her smile wickedly bright as she posed for the camera.

A knot formed in Eve's stomach, a tiny little seed that grew bigger, harder, as she studied every pixel of the photograph, of the way the woman was latched on to Jodi.

Her trance snapped when another magazine dropped onto the last, followed shortly by another.

Eve watched them land one at a time, entranced, enthralled, heat igniting anger, and jealousy chewing her insides like a Pac-Man. It didn't matter what she wore—jeans, slacks, nothing—Jodi was so enticing in every outfit. Her hair unkempt, those piercing jade eyes, she was impossibly sexy. It was easy to see what kept her agenda full, how she attracted the women.

Khandi dropped another and leaned back. "Are you pissed at me?"

Eve eyed her for several seconds, then looked at the cover. Jodi wore another tuxedo in this picture. Eve didn't have to see beneath the jacket to know what rested there. Her tongue had the pleasure of tasting every groove.

She concentrated on Jodi, on her dates, the way they stood beside each other. Jodi's vacant face.

Then she saw it. The delicate way her "date" rested her hand around her arm, in the crook of her elbow. That spark of jealousy whipped to life again, and Eve had to inhale to tap it back in place. She had no right to be jealous of Jodi, or the women she'd obviously fucked at the conclusion of their nights. But, dear God, she did. It made her crazy to think of someone else pumping beneath that tongue.

All of the magazines held the same similarities, all with Jodi as a date to someone well known or wealthy. Eve wasn't sure why she kept looking. She was riveted to every scene, every snapshot of Jodi's face, every pose.

It suddenly hit her something was off. Jodi's face was void of any emotion. It was lifeless. Not a single photo had captured a smile, grin, or smirk. Eve casually fanned the magazines out. Not one. She wasn't sure what it meant, if anything.

Her mind snapped back to their walk along the Thames. Eve had tucked her hand around Jodi's elbow, and she'd flinched. She'd felt it, wondered about it, but then Jodi had taken her hand, had woven their fingers together as if it were the most natural act in the world, and it *had* felt like the most natural thing in the world.

As quickly as she'd scanned over the covers for a smile, she reversed back over them. Not one showed her holding hands either. Her arm, elbow, bicep, but nothing as personal as linking fingers with another. Their poses were clinical.

Had Jodi allowed them to touch her at night's end, out of sight of the paparazzi, behind closed doors?

Shocked at the question, the jealousy, at that knot swelling once again, Eve scooped the magazines into a pile and pushed them toward Khandi. "What does this have to do with the fact that you're supposed to be getting me shots from the latest group of models?"

Khandi looked stunned. "No gasp of shock? No screaming at me for not telling you?" She leaned toward Eve. "Why do I smell something rotten?"

Eve took a deep breath. "Khandi, I knew."

Khandi's eyes widened and she slammed back. "What? You knew the whole time and didn't tell your bestie?"

"You're seriously chastising me for not telling you?" Eve chuckled. "When you obviously knew *long* before I did?"

Khandi hung her head, pursed her lips into a pouty face, and batted her long lashes. "But, boss, you were so…love-struck."

Eve laughed. "I might have been a few things, stupid being number one, but love-struck wasn't in the equation."

"Yeah. Right. Whatever." Khandi tossed another magazine on the desk. "Look at this one. Five months ago. You won't find her anywhere."

Thankfully, this one was void of Jodi's gorgeous face.

She tossed another on top. "And this one, three months ago. No Jodi."

Another landed. "Or this one, two months ago."

One more landed with a thump. "And last month's issue. Nothing, nada, zilch. She's nowhere in any of them."

"I'm assuming you're going to get to the point before I turn forty?"

Khandi huffed. "She ducked out because of you. Don't you get it? She loves you."

Eve's heart warmed and careened in her chest. Then anger bubbled that her heart had done anything at all. She pushed out of her chair. "That's it! I'm calling your pharmacist. No more over-the-counter medication for you." She walked around the desk and gently urged Khandi toward the door. "Take your tail back to that computer and get me those shots printed before I start looking for a new assistant. And for the love of God, cancel your subscriptions to the London tabloids. It's deranging that brain of yours."

Khandi stalled at the threshold. "Fine, I'll go, but you have to read this one. Amelia sent it for you. Hot off the press." She shoved the last magazine into Eve's hands.

"Wait! What? Amelia? From *Ruccar*? Why are you talking to her?" Eve had avoided contacting her about the new itinerary, too afraid she'd mention Jodi's name. She could have easily handed the task to Khandi, but dumping her normal chores on anyone else made her feel like a loser.

A devilish smile washed over Khandi's face. "Oh, we're tight like this now." She crossed her fingers, proving to Eve that she'd been right to keep the last bit of the secrets to herself, that Jodi was Lexi. "We have dibs on which of you is more miserable."

Khandi started down the hall and yelled over her shoulder. "Page thirty-two. Read it! Jodi looks hot! Or should I call her Lexi?"

Eve gasped and slammed the door. Was there one morsel of her fucking life that someone else didn't know?

And miserable? Bullshit! She wasn't miserable. Misery couldn't be further from what she felt. She stomped back to her desk, trying to reassure herself of that fact, and dropped into the chair with a huff.

Tonight, she'd venture to the lesbian bar. She'd snatch up the first willing butch she laid her eyes on, and she'd fuck her until the sun kissed the morning sky. *Miserable, my ass.*

Curiosity getting the better of her, she checked to make sure Khandi wasn't standing outside the office glass window, then thumbed to the page. There was Jodi, leaning against the building of her condo, the very building where she'd fucked Eve over and over. Her insides clenched. Dammit. It was unsettling how her body completely had a mind of its own.

She started reading the article, strongly aware that she was hanging on every word, that her heart was ripping and tears were streaming down her face.

❖

Jodi stood on the sidewalk looking up at the mirrored high-rise looming against the London skyline like a magnificent giant. In that building, she'd made a fresh beginning. Inside those walls, she'd made love and lost the woman of her dreams.

And now she was ready to leave it behind, in the caring hands of its new owners, people who would turn every floor and room into a homeless facility. She'd only minutes ago signed the final paperwork and handed over the deed. It was done, complete.

Within a year, once all the tenants had left, every homeless teenager would have a place to go, no questions asked, for a roof over their head, out of the cold, away from the hands that meant them harm. They would never go hungry or be afraid.

Their security was her gift, in honor of her parents, in honor of herself.

Physically tired of the memories, of always remembering, and ready to move ahead, Jodi glanced down the street. People rushed by her, umbrellas open, oblivious to the idiot standing in the rain, unprotected from the cold drops.

It was here, in the cleansing rain, where the real magic was at work, washing away all vestiges of the bad. Not the building or the bright white apartment that would form the social hub of the project. Her past, the hurt, the horrible memories, it all faded with the dampening drops, made everything fresh and new, crisp, clear.

This city had been her home for a very long time. It'd also been her nightmare and her dreams.

Now it was time to leave it all behind. It was time to move on. Time to start brand new.

Her savings would take her anywhere her heart desired. The world was now her playground. She could do anything, be anyone. Never again would she be that escort, or a sex operator, and never again would she allow a day to pass her by that she wasn't looking for love. That home, that fence, that garage, and that damn dog, she was going to have it all. All she had to do was be free, open, and wait.

The one would come. And Jodi would be ready for her this time, her eyes, mind, and heart wide open.

Until then, she'd breathe. And take one day at a time.

With a sigh, she started down the street and immediately thought of Eve. Thanks to Eve, she'd find all she desired. Witnessing Eve run from love had shown Jodi just how desperate she was to find it. How ready she was to own it.

Fifteen minutes later, she came to the studio. She recalled the last time she'd seen Eve's face. Nothing had ever torn the seam of her heart apart like Eve's broken expression had. Her confusion, her hurt, had jerked at Jodi's emotions like nothing else.

What she wouldn't give to have a woman like her, feisty, strong-willed, yet tender and vulnerable, even if only Jodi knew that soft side while the world knew the hardcore businesswoman.

Jodi knew just how vulnerable, just how fragile, Eve had been. She'd heard it through every whimper and cry.

Eve had been the one. She hated knowing that, possibly more than anything. Knowing that it could never be. That it never could have been.

She ducked under an awning and glanced across the street, at the restaurant where she'd walked away from Eve, with all her pride intact, and her head held high.

It wasn't Eve who'd prompted this change, who'd made her burn her little black book.

Those decisions had come from within Jodi's heart. Eve might have played a tiny role, might have had a little to do with some choices, with Jodi's wide-eyed decisions, but she wasn't the deciding factor.

Fact was, she'd stayed too long, outlived her escort days. She'd bypassed her comfort zone to feel safe, had acquired savings far beyond her needs. There was nothing to run from anymore.

She wanted love above all else now, and witnessing Eve living for only the fantasy, dodging love's clutches, made her see just how badly she wanted that dream, that missing link.

Thank you, Eve. Jodi pulled her shoulders forward and started walking again.

The rain bounced off her loafers and her feet were cold. She'd walk the last few blocks to the hotel, order room service, and sink into a hot bath, in the exact room Eve and her comrades had stayed in. The royal suite.

She wasn't sure what had possessed her to stay there, with Amelia pleading for her to take the spare bedroom in her house. It was sweet, but right now, she didn't want Amelia's pity. She wanted to be alone, to think, to recharge and pick up the pieces.

And she'd done that. One tiny step at a time, starting with the splash of her cell phone into the river. She'd disconnected the sex line, had a glass of wine while her little black book burned in the kitchen sink, and now, she'd given away her home. As heavy as it seemed, she was ready to lift her chin and step into the future.

Plus, lying across the bed where Eve had lain, thinking about the phone snuggled against her ear while she'd masturbated to Lexi's words, well, it was stupid, but it had given her new hope. That she'd find someone who didn't live for the safety net of a pipe dream. Especially when Jodi could be all the fantasy she ever wanted.

A few more weeks getting her funds in order, selling off a portion of her storage unit, and she'd set out to somewhere. Hell, maybe she'd use the globe as a dartboard to choose her destination. It truly didn't matter.

Amelia would be traveling very soon, setting out on her new career. It annoyed her that Amelia would be so close to Eve, witnessing her frantically setting things in order, always in charge with that sharp tongue. But she couldn't be more proud of Amelia. She deserved all the joy and happiness her new position could bring her, even if that meant she'd be exactly where Jodi had wanted to be, so fucking close to Eve.

With a sigh, she walked a little faster. No one else would ever know the true Eve like Jodi did. She'd gotten to the deep part of her, the soft center. The Eve that no one else had ever and might never see.

She also didn't regret not telling Eve the truth. Had she confessed earlier, when Eve was wide open for the truth, Eve would have been gone long before she got the chance to know her. Things always happened for a reason. Jodi knew what that reason was—to cut herself loose from a past she'd been clinging to out of habit, out of desperation to survive, even if survival was no longer part of the equation.

When her new cell phone chirped, she ducked beneath another awning and shook the rain from her hair. She withdrew the device from her pocket to study the display but didn't recognize the number.

An eerie sensation shot down her spine. There was no sex line, no Lexi, or a reason to drop her voice into a deep Brit accent. No clients. No Eve.

She clicked the Ignore button. That life was gone. And no one other than Amelia had the number.

It immediately rang again. Same unfamiliar number.

She flipped it open and held it to her ear. "Hello?"

"What are you wearing, Jodi?"

Her heart jammed tight and she stepped back against the brick building for support. God, how could that petite little thing still have that kind of impact with her voice alone?

"Eve."

"Trust me, you're not wearing Eve."

Jodi smiled as the raindrops swelled against the sidewalk, landing in large splats. "How'd you get this number?"

"Well, you see, I met this egotistical millionaire named Zara in London years ago. I explained how I was looking for a fantasy because love just didn't work for me. She gave me your number, said you were the complete package."

"Ah. I've always wondered." Jodi made a mental note to send an anonymous bouquet of roses to Zara, if only to know the self-centered wench would drive herself insane trying to find her secret admirer.

"But something screwy is going on with that phone line."

"Yeah. Something like that." Jodi hooked her thumb through the loop of her jeans and kicked her foot against the building.

"So I had to finagle a few favors owed me, and voila, here I am."

"I see." Jodi watched people's feet against the concrete, how the water splattered around their shoes, anything not to think about Eve, naked, arched, and coming.

Jodi knew she should hang up, to sever the connection. God knew she ought to. But she couldn't.

She was over Eve. Her heart told her so. But hearing her voice clenched something tight in her gut.

"I still don't know what you're wearing."

"A tie-dyed muumuu and orange high-top sneakers."

Eve laughed and Jodi squeezed her eyes shut. She missed that laugh.

"I'm trying my best to imagine what Lexi would say right now. Something erotic, for sure."

"There's no Lexi."

"Sure there is. Jodesy Alexis Connelly."

Oh God. She'd read the article. Jodi was positive Eve would never set eyes on the interview with her heart, her fears, her demons, all poured out over the pages.

She'd laid it all out, from traveling the map as a military brat, her father's death, her mother's death, to being alone on foreign soil, without a single person to turn to. How the road had led her to being a phone sex operator, eventually becoming a high-priced escort. There was no glamour in being a whore, only shame, only seclusion, and not once in the interview did she condone her actions. It was the only way for her. The only refuge.

It was Amelia who'd told her to start writing a book, a written record so that the world could learn something from her adventures. It was Amelia who set up the interview with a publicist, followed shortly by a magazine reporter. It was Amelia who'd found the charity and a project manager to set Jodi's wishes in motion.

It was always Amelia. Her heart, her friend, her only family. The only one who ever cared.

"Jodi."

"What…Eve?" Jodi opened her eyes.

"I want to kiss you in the rain."

Jodi chuckled. "You hate the rain."

"I do. I can't deny it. That doesn't change the fact that I want to kiss you in it."

"Eve, why are…what are you doing?" *Why are you doing this to me? I'm broken, healing. Can't you hear that? Trying to move on with life, trying to be normal. Dammit, please don't do this.*

Eve stepped out of the restaurant where she'd watched Jodi from the tinted window. Truth was, she didn't know what the fuck she was doing.

What she did know was the only woman to touch her deeply,

mentally and physically, was standing across the street. All she had to do was go get her.

Letting Jodi walk out those restaurant doors had been a mistake. She knew that now. Eve hadn't been looking for love. Quite the opposite, actually. But there it'd been, wrapped deliciously in billboard attire, a tight body beneath, exactly how she'd painted the fantasy woman in her mind. Of course, there was that little issue about her being a paid escort, and all the reasons that pushed her there. Eve didn't care. She didn't give a shit where Jodi had come from, or how she'd gotten there. She was here now, a constant ache in Eve's heart, a permanent fixture in her mind. Eve had no desire to fix the twist in her. She wanted to be twisted with her.

Like an idiot, she'd allowed Jodi to get free. She wouldn't make the same mistake twice.

"I wish I knew. God, I wish I knew." With a flick of the catch, Eve opened the umbrella, checked traffic, and darted across the street. Jodi was perched against the building farther along the block, her head pressed against the brick. She looked lonely, same as she had that night at the studio standing on the curb.

The rain had sealed Jodi's shirt and jacket against her body, her hair wet yet still incredibly sexy. She looked so forlorn with her shoulders tilted forward. The sight made Eve swallow, made her heart throb uncontrollably. The pain of wanting, of longing, spread through her body like a wildfire. Eve knew how she felt, how disturbing that lack of control was. Right now, she wanted to lose it all for one kiss in this rain.

Jodi was the most gorgeous thing Eve had ever seen. So in tune with all Eve wanted, needed, desired, in and out of bed. She was perfect in every way possible.

Eve stepped behind a couple holding hands and thought of her mother, their conversation only weeks ago.

"Mom, why did you settle for a family instead of a career?"

"Love."

"Love? Just like that, poof? All for love?"

"Just like that. One glance at your tiny little face, my innocent angel, and I fell in love."

"Me? I'm the reason you became that carpooling, snot-wiping mom, with no life of her own?"

"No life? Who said I didn't have a life?"

"Well, you didn't. Really."

"Sweetie, there is nothing more important than your family, your children, love. There's nothing above it. Love is the only reality."

Her mother had said she'd know when love snagged her. It would make her crazy stupid, make her heart feel things it never could before, and make her think of nothing else but that person, desperate to be near her, even if that connection was only her voice.

Her mother was right. She knew. God, how she knew. She felt it, deep in her being, rushing through her veins like a breakaway horse.

If she had to beg, she would. If she had to crawl around on this puddle-filled sidewalk on her hands and knees, she would. Right now she didn't give a shit what it took to get one kiss from Jodi, in this wet, cold rain. She wasn't above any of it.

But she was above giving up.

Eve slowed her steps when only fifty feet separated her from Jodi. "Now, about that kiss."

Jodi's hollow laugh echoed in Eve's ear. "Sorry, sexy. You can't afford me." She pushed off the wall and started walking again. The rain instantly slicked her hair down.

Eve liked hearing her voice lift. Jodi had been ashamed long enough, no matter how high she held that head. "Hmm. Three thousand, was it?"

"That was then. And this is Eve Harris. The price just jumped to six grand."

"My, my. Aren't you a little conceited? Guess that means you'll have to set me up a tab. Or we could work it out in, say, sweat equity?"

Jodi's steps quickened and she moved through the people with ease.

As for Eve, she'd already clashed umbrellas with two people, both who gave her an apology instead of the scowl every New Yorker would have thrown her way.

Another block of phone silence and Eve was out of breath trying to keep up.

"You're killing me, Jodi."

Jodi stopped so fast Eve had to skid to a halt and practically took out the bar holding the awning up with her umbrella.

"Eve, what the hell do you want from me? I think we know what you're looking for. What I can't give you."

"I want a damn kiss." Eve walked forward, closing the distance. "Can't you give me that?"

Jodi lifted her arm and let it drop over her head. "No, Eve. I can't. Please. Stop."

Eve did and smiled. She liked this little cat-and-mouse game. She'd have to pick fights more often. God, the make-up sex was going to be incredible.

"Raise the edge of that grotesque muumuu, Jodi. Touch yourself."

"Eve..."

"Can you feel me? My lips hot against your clit, my fingers buried deep?" Eve walked slower, still too far for Jodi to hear her. "Or you, behind me, watching me, watching you, your reflection fucking me."

"Fuck. Stop!" Jodi stopped in front of the hotel where Eve had spent a week, minus her nights wrapped warmly in Jodi's arms, her body weak, sore, and satisfied.

"Make me stop, Jodi." Eve moved forward, twenty feet. Fifteen. Ten. "Kiss me. Shut me up."

Jodi whipped around, searching the sidewalk, and then her gaze landed like a bomb on Eve.

Every part of Eve's body awakened. Her heart slammed and her stomach clenched. God only knew what her insides were doing. Churning, slicking, tightening, all with only a stare from those glittering eyes.

Eve struggled forward, afraid her knees would give out like a pathetic damsel in distress, and stopped within five feet of Jodi.

Jodi looked from her face, down to her new boots, and then back up. "What are...why are you here?"

"Look, I'm not good at this dating stuff. Never have been." Eve drew in a breath, terrified she'd fuck this up. Crawling, groveling, and begging, seemed so much easier than explaining than apologizing. "I'm stupid. Okay?"

"Eve. Don't."

Eve shook her head and held up her hand. "I'm not here to get down on bended knee, Jodi, or declare my undying love." She took one step. "But I can't get you out of my head. I miss you. All of you. Both of you."

Jodi could only stare, her mind swallowing every word, their silent meaning. It wasn't the declaration she would have hoped for, but coming from Eve, it was practically perfect.

"I can't be your fantasy, Eve."

Eve took the last step. "You already are. Now shut the hell up and kiss me already."

The umbrella landed on the sidewalk as Eve pressed her body against Jodi's. Their lips met and the rain poured over them.

About the Author

Larkin Rose lives in a "blink and you've missed it" town in the beautiful state of South Carolina. She and her partner share seven kids, three ferocious Chihuahuas, one lucky cat, five beautiful grandsons, and finally, a granddaughter.

Her writing career began four years ago when the voices in her head wouldn't stop their constant chatter. After ruling out multiple personalities and hitting the keyboard, a writer emerged.

The loud voices of characters remain. The clatter of keys continues. The birth of erotic creations carries on.

Books Available From Bold Strokes Books

Blood Hunt by LL Raand. In the second Midnight Hunters Novel, Detective Jody Gates, heir to a powerful Vampire clan, forges an uneasy alliance with Sylvan, the Wolf Were Alpha, to battle a shadow army of humans and rogue Weres, while fighting her growing hunger for human reporter Becca Land. (978-1-60282-209-2)

Loving Liz by Bobbi Marolt. When theater actor Marty Jamison turns diva and Liz Chandler walks out on her, Marty must confront a cheating lover from the past to understand why life is crumbling around her. (978-1-60282-210-8)

Kiss the Rain by Larkin Rose. How will successful fashion designer Eve Harris react when she discovers the new woman in her life, Jodi, and her secret fantasy phone date, Lexi, are one and the same? (978-1-60282-211-5)

Sarah, Son of God by Justine Saracen. In a story within a story within a story, a transgendered beauty takes us through Stonewall-rioting New York, Venice under the Inquisition, and Nero's Rome. (978-1-60282-212-2)

Sleeping Angel by Greg Herren. Eric Matthews survives a terrible car accident only to find out everyone in town thinks he's a murderer—and he has to clear his name even though he has no memories of what happened. (978-1-60282-214-6)

Dying to Live by Kim Baldwin & Xenia Alexiou. British socialite Zoe Anderson-Howe's pampered life is abruptly shattered when she's taken hostage by FARC guerrillas while on a business trip to Bogota, and Elite Operative Fetch must rescue her to complete her own harrowing mission. (978-1-60282-200-9)

Indigo Moon by Gill McKnight. Hope Glassy and Godfrey Meyers are on a mercy mission to save their friend Isabelle after she is attacked by a rogue werewolf—but does Isabelle want to be saved from the sexy wolf who claimed her as a mate? (978-1-60282-201-6)

Parties in Congress by Colette Moody. Bijal Rao, Indian-American moderate Independent, gets the break of her career when she's hired to work on the congressional campaign of Janet Denton—until she meets her remarkably attractive and charismatic opponent, Colleen O'Bannon. (978-1-60282-202-3)

Black Fire: Gay African-American Erotica, edited by Shane Allison. *Black Fire* celebrates the heat and power of sex between black men: the rude B-boys and gorgeous thugs, the worshippers of heavenly ass, and the devoutly religious in their forays through the subterranean grottoes of the down-low world. (978-1-60282-206-1)

The Collectors by Leslie Gowan. Laura owns what might be the world's most extensive collection of BDSM lesbian erotica, but that's as close as she's gotten to the world of her fantasies. Until, that is, her friend Adele introduces her to Adele's mistress Jeanne—art collector, heiress, and experienced dominant. With Jeanne's first command, Laura's life changes forever. (978-1-60282-208-5)

Breathless, edited by Radclyffe and Stacia Seaman. Bold Strokes Books romance authors give readers a glimpse into the lives of favorite couples celebrating special moments "after the honeymoon ends." Enjoy a new look at lesbians in love or revisit favorite characters from some of BSB's best-selling romances. (978-1-60282-207-8)

Breaker's Passion by Julie Cannon. Leaving a trail of broken hearts scattered across the Hawaiian Islands, surf instructor Colby Taylor is running full speed away from her selfish actions years earlier until she collides with Elizabeth Collins, a stuffy, judgmental college professor who changes everything. (978-1-60282-196-5)

Justifiable Risk by V.K. Powell. Work is the only thing that interests homicide detective Greer Ellis until internationally renowned journalist Eva Saldana comes to town looking for answers in her brother's death—then attraction threatens to override duty. (978-1-60282-197-2)

Nothing But the Truth by Carsen Taite. Sparks fly when two top-notch attorneys battle each other in the high-risk arena of the courtroom, but when a strange turn of events turns one of them from advocate to witness, prosecutor Ryan Foster and defense attorney Brett Logan join forces in their search for the truth. (978-1-60282-198-9)